Track Down El Salvador

A Brad Jacobs Thriller

Book 6

SCOTT CONRAD

PUBLISHED BY:
Scott Conrad
2nd Edition © April 2019

A Brad Jacobs Thriller Series by Scott Conrad:

TRACK DOWN AFRICA – BOOK 1

TRACK DOWN ALASKA – BOOK 2

TRACK DOWN AMAZON – BOOK 3

TRACK DOWN IRAQ – BOOK 4

TRACK DOWN BORNEO – BOOK 5

TRACK DOWN EL SALVADOR – BOOK 6

TRACK DOWN WYOMING – BOOK 7

Visit the author at: ScottConradBooks.com

"All right, they're on our left, they're on our right, they're in front of us, they're behind us...they can't get away this time."

Lewis B. Chesty Puller, USMC. The Battle at the "Frozen Chosen" Korean War – 1950.

Table of Contents

ONE

Day 0–4 days, San Benito, San Salvador, El Salvador

Thirty men dressed in black with an odd gold emblem embroidered on their sleeves descended on the tiny hamlet outside Soyapango with blood in their eyes. They were loaded for bear, armed to the teeth with suppressed automatic weapons, sidearms, fragmentation grenades, and explosives. Everything, in short, needed to start, and finish, a small war. Automatic weapons fire from unsuppressed weapons could be heard throughout the sleepy little village, and terrified residents raced out into the streets to see what was going on only to be cut down where they stood, open-mouthed and shocked.

Men, women, children, small and large animals, all were eliminated dispassionately and left where they lay. The village elder, a man who had spoken out against the actions of the warlord known only as "El Caiman", had been dragged from his bed and, along with every member of his immediate family, been taken out into the village square to watch the horror show. The faces of the gang of black-clad men forcing them to watch showed no expression as the blood of the innocent villagers ran freely in the streets.

When the atrocity was over, the elder's eyes were taped open and he was forced to watch the execution of his own wife and children. After the dreadful act was completed, he was forced to his knees in front of the leader of the attackers. The leader silently placed a heavy, solid gold medallion around the old man's scrawny neck. The medallion matched the embroidered caiman on the leader's shirt. Then the attackers evaporated into the shadows, leaving the elder kneeling in the center of the obliterated hamlet. The message was clear enough. El Caiman would tolerate no opposition of any kind.

* * *

"I want the girls alive, understood?"

The tall man nodded his understanding. El Caiman did not like to be interrupted.

"I want the servants and security staff thoroughly cowed, but leave Feng be. Daubert is on duty in the safe room tonight, and he's one of ours. At precisely 2135 hours tonight he will shut down all exterior security devices. After that, it's up to you to execute the operation just the way we rehearsed it. Any questions, Lucien?"

"No sir!"

"Good. I'm counting on you, Lucien. I know you won't let me down." The warlord turned away, his mind on other matters, the tall man forgotten.

* * *

The team of ten men was dressed all in black, and they wore thin balaclavas that would roll down to cover their faces when they reached their objective for no other reason than to strike terror into the hearts of the villagers. They were not in the least concerned about concealing their identities. Everyone in El Salvador would recognize the gold caiman embroidered on the left sleeve of their black shirts anyway, it was the well-known emblem of the most feared man in all El Salvador, El Caiman. They made their way on foot after offloading from the black carryalls in absolute stealth up the steep slope of El Boquerón, the volcano on the far western edge of San Salvador in the San Benito subdivision, under the cover of darkness, toward the impressive three-story mansion of Feng Jingguo. Feng was the titular head of Feng Industries, a quasi-private appliance manufacturing company located in San Salvador under the auspices of China's efforts to expand their economy in the face of impending tariffs in the U.S. and their anticipation of a trade war.

The exclusive neighborhood was patrolled by private security forces and the Policia Nacional Civil, also known as PNC, but those forces chose to ignore the presence of El Caiman's men. The threat of repercussions alone would have been sufficient to deter the security forces from interfering with the black-clad men, but the fact that the men were fairly bristling with heavy weaponry was an even greater deterrent.

The team's mission was to abduct Feng's teenage daughters from the mansion and take them to El Caiman's estate, where the team members supposed El Caiman would decide what to do with them. The men were extremely well paid for their proficiency and expertise, and they knew that El Caiman wasn't paying them to be curious, he just expected results. He also wasn't known for tolerating failure. The penalties for failure did not bear thinking about.

Their instructions were clear: they were to abduct the girls as quietly as possible and then leave the mansion and its inhabitants in mortal terror. The owner, Feng, was not to be harmed. The men, all hand-picked from El Caiman's small army of mercenaries, were all highly trained and well-disciplined former non-commissioned officers of the Légion étrangère, the French Foreign Legion, and were led by former Adjudant-chef (Sergeant Major) Lucien Piccard. Piccard was the only member of the small army that knew El Caiman's real name. The two had served together in Chad and Northern Mali.

Piccard never uttered a word. He used hand signals to direct his troops when necessary once they had left the carryalls that had transported them to the base of El Boquerón. They then proceeded on foot to the mansion, a precaution Piccard believed necessary because of the lack of intelligence available and the unpredictability of the gang activity rampant in in modern San Salvador.

At 2130 hours, the team split up, one half hid on the side of the mansion and the other half raced around to the rear entrance. At 2134 hours, Lucien Piccard simply walked up to the front door and knocked. A minute, perhaps longer, passed before the door was answered by a butler in formal dress. Before the butler could object, Piccard slid his booted foot into the doorway and blew a single sharp blast on the whistle hanging on a lanyard around his neck.

The team at the back of the mansion kicked in the substantial rear door and entered at the same time the team from the side of the house blew past Piccard and entered the front. Every man kept an internal count, practiced countless times in training, as they secured the inside of the house. Piccard walked casually to the safe room and knocked three times then knocked twice more. He heard two shots fired in rapid succession inside the room and a second later the door was opened by a man with a familiar face.

"Make it look good, Piccard, but for God's sake do the left side. I still have trouble with my right side where I took that round in the ass in Kidal."

"If you had been in better shape that asshole would never have been able to shoot you," Piccard said as he casually removed a Beretta 92 FS from its holster and fired a single round into Daubert's left side.

"Jesus that hurts!"

"You will live, Daubert. It's only a scratch."

Daubert clapped a hand over the bloody hole in his side to stanch the bleeding. "It's more than a scratch *connard*!"

Piccard laughed, an unpleasant sound. "Just be glad I like you, Daubert. If I didn't I might have shot you in the head." He traded his Beretta for Daubert's identical piece and then turned and set about placing small shape charges on the outside of the door to make it appear as if the door had been blown open. He never bothered to check to see if Daubert had made it back inside the safe room before he detonated the charges.

He walked into the marble tiled foyer and waited with his arms crossed for the two teams to return. He noted with displeasure that the first team, the one that had gone upstairs to get the girls, was two beats off the count when they returned with their captives. His breath was taken away when he saw the younger sister, Feng Chu Hua if he remembered correctly, and he always did. The Chinese girl was exceptionally beautiful and very fragile looking. The older sister, Feng Meng, was coarser, a little chunky, and Piccard thought the girl must have had a different mother, perhaps a peasant woman. Shrugging his shoulders, Piccard looked up to see the second team approaching shoving Feng Jingguo, in restraints, ahead of them. They were right on the count.

"Take the restraints off," Piccard ordered. They were more for humiliation than for restraint in any event. One of the NCOs removed the restraints, none too gently.

"Why have you violated the sanctity of my home?" Feng demanded arrogantly.

Piccard gestured toward one of the black-clad figures, who immediately slapped the older sister so hard that her knees buckled and her head slammed into the foyer wall.

Feng started to move toward her but froze immediately when several automatic weapons were leveled at his belly. His forward motion stopped, but his eyes flashed furiously. Piccard took his Beretta out of its holster with practiced ease and nonchalantly shot the butler, who had been brought back into the foyer with Feng, in the forehead.

"The next word out of your mouth will cause the same thing to happen to one of your daughters," Piccard said drily. "I have nothing further to say to you and I have no need of a response." Feng showed the first signs of real distress and his eyes suddenly focused on the gold caiman on Piccard's sleeve.

Piccard reached into his pocket and removed a golden medallion exactly like the one given to the village elder earlier. He hung it around Feng's neck then, with a hand signal, indicated that the girls should be taken outside. "Trash the house," he ordered the others.

None of them noticed the small boy from the stable behind the mansion as he watched them leave unhurriedly, pushing the two girls down the long driveway in front of them. He had heard the gunshots and the noise of destruction inside the mansion. He was terrified, and he was smart enough to keep his mouth shut and remain unnoticed.

* * *

El Caiman's true identity was not known to the Salvadoran Government and in fact was known only to a handful of intelligence specialists in a couple of Western countries, including the United States. He was Simon Leclerc, actually a South African who was cashiered from the French Foreign Legion and imprisoned for committing hideous atrocities against non-combatants in Chad. With the aid of two former legionnaires, including Piccard, he escaped from prison and disappeared. A short time later, he turned up in El Salvador and ruthlessly began to make a name for himself. He became a "*transportista*" serving the local gangs and the drug cartels of Central and South America, who referred to him as "El Caiman" because he was as vicious and mindless as that reptile in the pursuit of his goals.

Frankly, he and the men he recruited scared the hell out of the gangs and cartels. Piccard and the other legionnaire who escaped with him formed the core of El Caiman's organization, which he kept relatively small. Over time, he became a kind of feudal overlord over the entire province.

El Caiman grew into a sort of local legend, considered by all concerned to be untouchable because of his swift and ferocious retaliation against even an imagined slight. He brutally eliminated anything or anyone even vaguely resembling competition or a threat of any kind. He destroyed the village earlier because the elder had discouraged the locals from cooperating with him. El Caiman chose to make an example of absolutely anyone who opposed him, his detractors dying badly, usually along with their family, in order to *décourager* les autres. No one who got in his sights was immune, from the lowliest villager to the highest government officials.

El Caiman's secret villa in the mountains outside Soyapango, an impenetrable fortress once owned (and subsequently commandeered after a swift all-out assault by El Caiman and his small army of former legionnaires and mercenaries that left no one alive inside the estate) by a Colombian drug lord. His reputation had grown so formidable that the Colombian cartels choose to overlook his usurpation of the estate... The man had a long reach.

Once the cartels washed their hands of El Caiman, the state and local governments were so intimidated by him that it was privately decided at the highest levels that the safest thing to be done was to provide armed security around his entire estate. The Policia Nacional Civil provided marked vehicles and uniformed officers to patrol the outer boundaries of the estate. The officers turned a blind eye to the comings and goings of El Caiman's men. Some things it was healthier not to see.

* * *

Chu Hua and Meng sat huddled together in the back seat of the carryall, ignored by their abductors.

"Are you hurt, Meng?" Chu Hua whispered. Meng shook her head no, her eyes widening with fear because her sister dared to break the silence, but the abductors paid them no mind.

"Where are they taking us?"

Meng's eyes narrowed and then focused on the left sleeve of one of the men sitting in the seat in front of them. Chu Hua was perplexed for just a moment until she realized what Meng was staring at—the gold caiman embroidered on the man's sleeve. As the younger sister, Chu Hua had led a sheltered life, but even she knew the significance of the symbol.

The other kids at the private high school she attended in San Benito spoke of El Caiman in hushed tones when they spoke of him at all. They shared chilling tales of the warlord's depredations that they had overheard when their parents thought they weren't listening, and the stories scared all but the brasher of the kids. Some of the loners actually admired the man and there was a small clique that called themselves "The Gators" though the two reptiles were not the same.

Chu Hua felt a cold chill sweep through her as the enormity of what had just happened registered with her. It had happened so fast that even the murder of Jorge, their butler, hadn't seemed real. The realization that the gory execution was not some sort of scene from a movie but had actually occurred made her sick to her stomach and she wanted to throw up. It would not occur to her until much later what might happen to her because of her youth and beauty, but it was weighing heavily on Meng's mind.

Meng harbored no illusions as to what had happened to them, and she feared more for her little sister than she did for herself. If she was lucky, Meng knew she would be ransomed back to her father. If she was unlucky she would be killed out of hand. She knew there was no chance at all for the hapless Chu Hua. Her baby sister had gotten her looks from their mother's side of the family, petite and fair and blessed with oh, so delicate features that would now become a curse. Meng was older and worldlier than her sister, and she almost hoped that they would both be killed so that Chu Hua would not be subjected to the horrors of violation that were surely to come next.

* * *

Piccard was having a difficult time focusing his thoughts. The younger girl, Chu Hua, had taken his breath away the moment he had seen her ... the picture El Caiman had given him at the beginning of his briefing had not done the young woman justice at all. He had been expecting the skinny, buck-toothed girl in the photo, which had obviously been taken some years before. The sloe-eyed beauty brought down by the upstairs team bore no resemblance at all to the photograph.

Piccard was a man of discriminating tastes when it came to women. He liked them young, and he liked them small and delicate ... and Chu Hua was all of that and more. If he remembered correctly, it had been a very long time since he had been around any Chinese people, Chu Hua was the Mandarin word for chrysanthemum, and the flower's name described the girl perfectly.

He shook his head in an effort to clear his mind. Whatever El Caiman had in mind for the young flower, it would not be pretty. Piccard had some ideas of his own, and for the first time since he had met El Caiman, he was wishing he had the nerve to buck the man's will. Chu Hua was a precious treasure, and Piccard wanted her for himself more than he had ever wanted anything in his life.

TWO

Day 0–1 year, NSA Headquarters Building, Fort Meade, Maryland

Felicity Marie Highsmith had earned her first doctorate from MIT at the ripe old age of sixteen. A child prodigy, she had earned her second doctorate by the time she was eighteen. Snapped up by the National Security Agency (NSA), she spent twenty-one years with the organization, the last eleven coordinating highly classified intelligence between all the intelligence agencies and departments of the US government. At the age of thirty-nine, against the wishes and concerted efforts of her superiors, Felicity retired, tired of the games and the bullshit of the Washington D.C. bureaucracy, especially after she discovered that the U.S. government was unofficially endorsing a rogue character in El Salvador operating under the alias "El Caiman" by turning a blind eye to his atrocities and refusing an unofficial request from the El Salvadorian government official to intervene.

Her exit interview, which her direct supervisor conducted personally, was a bit odd.

"I've tried everything I know to get you to stay, Fly (the nickname had seemed a natural fit from the beginning, being both a contraction of her first name and a reference to her diminutive stature). So what are you going to do with yourself now? Are you going to stay in Arlington?" She owned a two-story brownstone in one of the oldest residential neighborhoods in Arlington, Virginia, which she had purchased for a song and lovingly restored herself over the years.

"Sorry John. I've had my fill of D.C. I grew up on a small ranch near Dallas that my folks left to me when Dad passed away a few years back. I'm going to sell the brownstone and go home. I miss the horses and I miss the people."

"The ranch house, has it been closed up since your dad passed?"

"Yes, it just didn't seem right to rent it out, so I've been paying someone to keep an eye on the place. I learned enough to do most of the repairs from working on my brownstone over the years, and I'll have to start from scratch with the stock, but it's honest work and I'll enjoy it."

"It could get awfully boring out there in the country alone after being here at the center of everything for so long."

She laughed then, loud and long. "Washington isn't the center of everything, Walter, people here just think it is. Sometimes I think the people here inside the Beltway forget that. I'm ready to get away from you Looneytunes and out among the real people of this country again."

Walter Driscoll's smile faltered a bit at that, but he reached into the center drawer of his desk and removed a thick manila folder.

"Just in case you get bored, Fly, I've taken the liberty of collecting a few bits and pieces of intel you have shown a particular interest in ... just in case you decide to keep your hand in the game. You know we occasionally need an outside consultant, and it's a way to augment your retirement check." He gave her a mildly reproachful look. "You realize you could have drawn a much higher percentage of your salary had you stayed another year or two."

"I know, Walter," she said, reaching for the folder but not opening it. "I just can't stand staying here another minute watching you guys ignore that asshole down in El Salvador."

"Now Fly, you know our hands are tied..."

"That crap never stopped any of you guys before," she said hotly. "All the way back before my time,

Teheran, Nicaragua, Ethiopia, hell, even friendly countries ... like Israel. You guys interfere whenever and wherever you like! Why stop now? This guy is the devil incarnate."

Driscoll had the good grace to blush. Then he grimaced and forged ahead, though his voice was lowered to a whisper. "There are a few members of the Senate, I'm not naming names, who will do anything ... anything at all ... to take this administration down."

Felicity opened her mouth for an angry retort, but Driscoll raised his hand to ward it off.

"Fly, you've been around this town long enough to know where the real power lies, but you don't understand just how far their reach extends. Sure, I could go to the president with this, or I could leak it to the press, but I would face termination if I did, and I'm not talking about getting fired, I'm talking termination with extreme prejudice."

Felicity opened her mouth again to deride him, but then it struck her that Walter wasn't kidding. She had known him since the first day she had come to work for NSA, and she knew his tells. Walter was deadly serious. She shut her mouth and sat back in the chair.

"Hell," he continued, "if they even find out I've given you this folder I'll be worm food."

Curious, Felicity opened the folder and quickly scanned the redacted reports inside. Her mouth formed a moue of disgust. Driscoll was so out of touch with his own subordinates. The reports he had assembled were from other agencies, but they were based on reports she had forwarded to them. There was nothing in them that she hadn't researched personally.

"What do you expect me to do with these, Walter?"

Driscoll handed her a three-by-five card with a name and address hand printed on one side.

"When you get to Dallas, get in touch with this guy. I think you might find him useful. He runs an ... interesting ... business."

Felicity was curious, but she knew she was not going to get anything else from the man who, until today, had been her boss.

* * *

At age forty, Felicity still had a youthful look and was often mistaken for a twenty-year-old. Only the skin on her throat and her hands gave any indication of her true age. Usually she wore her shoulder length brown hair in a ponytail. She had large brown eyes and an exceptionally pretty face.

The file folder Driscoll gave her had gone into a box that she'd shoved into the darkest corner of her bedroom closet as soon as she'd unpacked when she arrived back at the little forty-acre ranchette where she had spent her childhood years with her parents. Her Washington wardrobe had been carefully packed away and stored in the loft of the barn as soon as she'd made her first shopping trip to the cattleman's supply store in Decatur, Texas. She'd purchased four pairs of Levis, some lace-up Roper boots, and an assortment of western shirts and then talked with a salesman who remembered her from her childhood visits with her dad. Truly relaxed for the first time in years, Felicity chatted with the older man for more than an hour, just reminiscing.

An hour after she left the store, she drove her Subaru Forester into the barn next to her father's ancient Ford pickup and covered it with a tarp. She raised the hood on the old truck and walked over to the workbench where all her dad's tools remained in their places, just the way he'd left them. It took her a couple of hours to charge the battery, change the points and plugs, and give the battery a quick charge, but she felt a surge of pleasure as she did the familiar tasks.

For a year she worked on fixing up the house, getting the barn in order, and going to auctions to replenish the tack room, and of course, carefully selecting horses to buy. Feeding, training and riding the horses, and life on the ranch eased her soul more than she had ever dreamed possible, but still there was something missing in her life. She tried dating for a while. The rugged, manly cowboys were definitely a bit of a turn-on at first, but even though the men were of a type she admired, there was something missing in them too. She had no idea what it was she was looking for or why these cowboys didn't have it.

At the end of a year she had returned the ranchette to its former glory, and she was very pleased with herself. There was only one thing wrong. The ranch and the horses were not enough of a challenge.

Felicity found that she missed her work. Not the Washington folderol but the work itself. The box containing the manila folder Driscoll had given her came out of the closet, as well as the three-by-five card.

Two days later, she began work on converting one of the bunkhouses into one of the most sophisticated intelligence gathering and research facilities in the State of Texas. The bunkhouse became a computer center, where she established links through "backdoors" to the systems she helped create over the years. She started keeping track of ongoing operations to which she was no longer authorized access.

Over the years Felicity had built up many official and not-so-official contacts in the intelligence world, one of whom was a Chinese gentleman living and working in El Salvador...

THREE

Day 0–1 year, The "Manor House", northwest of Dallas, Texas

"Oh, come on, why in the hell would I want to attend a Cattleman's Association ball?"

Brad Jacobs, a 6'2", green-eyed man with a blond military style buzz cut and a muscular build, had often been told he looked a lot like Brad Pitt. He was no movie star though. Brad had joined the Marines at 18 years of age, just out of high school. It seemed a natural progression for him, his father had been a career Marine who was killed at the end of the Gulf War during Operation Desert Storm while serving under General Norman Schwarzkopf. Brad was proud of his father and proud of what the Marines stood for.

At forty-two, Brad was as American as apple pie. He had a lantern jaw and a look of self confidence in his eyes that came from a core of inner strength.

A core built from the courage of facing the toughest obstacles life could throw at him. He lived by a code and expected everyone else to do the same.

"Some of those cattlemen are richer than Croesus, Brad. They own extensive properties in Central and South America, and some are even expanding into Africa. Just the kind of men who are going to need your services sooner or later." Willona Ving had become the defacto treasurer by dint of the management skills she had shown over the years, making Mason Ving, Brad's closest friend, a millionaire even though the man was only a non-commissioned officer in the United States Marine Corps.

"I want to go, Brad!" Vicky Chance draped her arms around Brad's neck and pressed herself close against his back. Vicky was very tall and deceptively slender, with small, firm breasts. Her short, red hair, green eyes, long legs and flirty personality assured that every man in her general vicinity was captivated by her wherever she went.

Looks, however, can be deceiving. Vicky was a former I.C.E. Agent for Homeland Security, investigating child exploitation and trafficking in the Southern Cone, Central and South America. Before that, she had been a Warrant Officer (CWO3) in the United States Marine Corps Criminal Investigation Division (USMC C.I.D.) She had hooked up with Brad and Team Dallas in Mexico and earned her spurs in a gritty mission to the Amazon Basin.

"You really want to go hang around and socialize with a bunch of cattle barons and listen to a buttload of inane prattle, baby?"

"A girl likes to dress up now and then, Brad, and I love shopping for a new dress almost as much as I like sex."

Brad heaved a sigh of resignation. Vicky could be very persuasive when she got an idea in her head, and when she and Willona ganged up on him she was an unstoppable force. The shopping trip would be expensive, but Team Dallas was very flush after that last mission and it wasn't going to hurt ... much. He grinned as he thought about the dress Vicky would pick out. Dallas had some major couturiers, and Vicky was absolutely certain to pick out something outrageously revealing to wear. The woman certainly enjoyed being the center of attention.

* * *

"I ain't gonna forget this, Brad." Mason Ving stared into a triple mirror with an aggravated look on his broad face. "This gonna cost you big time, brother. I ain't payin' for this monkey suit, an' you are goin' to take me out an' buy me breakfast after all this."

Mason Ving, a massive black man with skin so dark it looked blue in the sunlight, was a loud, abrasive person; traits mitigated by the fact that he was outspoken, honest, honorable, confident, and virtually always happy.

He was born and grew up in the ghettos of New Orleans and his mother died when he was just twelve years old. He was the oldest of three brothers and had taken a paper route to help his dad put food on the table. He'd joined the Marine Corps when he was eighteen to escape a grinding life of poverty and to help support his family. He'd served with Brad in Afghanistan and Iraq, where he'd proven himself in battle over and over again. He and Brad were as close as any brothers alive.

When he left New Orleans as a teen, he'd never dreamed that someday he would own a home on a ranchette in an exclusive suburb outside Dallas or be married to the woman of his dreams and have two great kids of his own.

"Oh, so I get to pay for the monkey suits," Brad retorted.

"Yo' woman got me into this, you gotta pay for the monkey suits!"

Ving jumped when the tailor accidentally stabbed him with a straight pin and turned to scowl at the terrified little man. "I look like a pincushion to you?"

"No, no sir, sorry sir!" The diminutive tailor, already terrified of the monstrous black man, was babbling obsequiously and wringing his hands.

"Don't worry, Don, Ving hasn't bitten anybody this week."

"Yet..." Ving growled with a menacing scowl. He turned to Brad. "You gonna have to triple that order of bacon with my pancakes now, you understand?" Ving was known to a large number of Marine mess sergeants (and to his sons) as "The

Baconater" because of his appetite for bacon. The breakfast meat had been scarce and expensive in New Orleans when he was a boy, and he had often given his share to his younger brothers. When he got his first paycheck from the Corps, he had sent half home to his father and then gone straight to a restaurant off base and ordered bacon until they'd run out. For the first time in his life he'd eaten his fill of bacon.

"Let the guy alone, Ving, he's trying to find enough material to cover that big ass of yours so you won't embarrass me at that damned ball!"

"He can do it without sticking me fulla holes, Brad! That's FOUR orders of bacon ya owe me now!"

* * *

"Girl, every woman in Dallas is absolutely going to hate you if you wear that dress to the ball!"

Vicky smiled wickedly. "That's kinda what I had in mind, Willona!" The dress was the same sea-green color as her eyes, and it left her back bare almost down to her butt. The left sleeve was long, extending to her wrist, but the right sleeve was missing entirely, baring a great expanse of creamy skin and the under slope of one shapely breast. The fabric was thin and shimmery and clung to her like a second skin.

"You going to splurge on a pair of shoes to go with that crazy dress?"

Vicky smiled again. "But of course."

"Oh lord, you have that look in your eyes that says poor old Brad is going to pay dearly for this! Are we headed for the jewelry counter at Nieman-Marcus too?"

A throaty chuckle came from the sexy redhead's throat. "No. With this dress I don't need any jewelry."

"You got that right. Now I'm going to have to get a dress to make sure you don't shine me right out of the room. Ving is going to have a cow!"

* * *

"I think we might be a little overdressed," Brad mused, a delicate flute of expensive champagne in his hand.

"I think I'd rather have a cold beer," Ving retorted, lifting a bacon wrapped oyster from a serving platter held by a straight-laced waiter. He popped it into his mouth, chewing noisily, and admired the hand-made boots on a tall rangy man wearing a western cut suit and a broad-brimmed Stetson.

Brad's eyes ranged the ballroom, taking stock of the men he saw there. They were not at all what he had expected, even though he was a long time resident of Dallas. Instead of the paunchy, gaudily dressed men with glittering jewelry he had seen before at various public functions in Dallas society, these men had the hard, weathered look of men who had spent their lives in the saddle, men who knew cattle and knew their land from firsthand experience, from drinking coffee out of a tin cup around a campfire at the end of a long day herding cattle. In short, they looked a lot like Jared Smoot, a lanky, rawboned Texan who was a regular artist with a Barrett .50 sniper rifle. Jared was a quiet, reliable former Force Recon Marine who had served with Brad for many years and had been a charter member of Team Dallas.

The conversations being held quietly along the sides of the ballroom were more business oriented than social as far as Brad could tell from the snippets of conversation he could catch.

Brad turned his eyes back to the dance floor where Vicky was leaving her latest dance partner and coming towards him. He was as aware of the envious stares of the other men as he was of the jealous stares of the well-dressed women in the ballroom. Vicky was indeed a spectacular sight.

"These boys do love to dance," she murmured when she reached him. She held out one delicate hand and took his champagne flute from his and took a healthy sip.

"I think they just like getting close to you." He took her into his arms. "That dress is probably giving them the same ideas I'm having right now..."

"Ideas don't hurt anybody." She chuckled. "Besides, you're the only man here that's going to get to see me when I take it off..."

"I hate to admit it, but seeing you in that getup is worth the annoyance of having to endure this little soiree."

"Willona was right, Brad. Some of these men, maybe several, are going to need you and Team Dallas in the future. Look at this like a business deal because that's what it is," Vicky said seriously.

Brad grinned. “It may be, but it sure looks to me like you’re having a good time.”

“I am,” she said gaily as she left him when another well-dressed cowman asked her to dance.

Brad watched the guy twirl her around the floor for a moment and then turned to find himself face-to-face, or rather, chest-to-face, with a tiny brown-haired woman in a very sophisticated, elegant but understated black dress. She looked up into his eyes.

“You’re Brad Jacobs, aren’t you?” It was actually more of a statement than a question.

“Yes I am.” He cocked his head to one side and looked closely at her face. She looked more like a well-to-do librarian than a cattleman’s lady. “I’m afraid you have the advantage of me. Have we met?”

"No, not that I know of. I'm sorry, I've just retired from government service in D.C. I recognized you from your State Department file pictures."

"You worked for the State Department?"

"No." She waved a hand dismissively. "I worked in the Intelligence community, that's how I happened to see your files. Your Team Dallas has been involved in some pretty juicy stuff. You shouldn't be surprised that you've garnered some attention in Washington."

"To tell you the truth, I never really thought about it much."

"An operation like yours tends to step on a few toes now and then, Mr. Jacobs, you should keep that in mind. You've come perilously close to upsetting a few of the senators on the Armed Services Committee a couple of times, but so far you've been lucky."

"I guess we have. We usually don't take on anything that the government could handle on their own without causing a stir."

"That's true, but then you don't have any way of knowing if you're interfering with an ongoing clandestine operation or not, do you?"

Brad shook his head. "No, I guess we've been pretty lucky so far. He didn't know if this woman was aware of Vicky and Charlie and their Intelligence connections, but she already knew more than he was comfortable with so he wasn't volunteering a damned thing.

"You should probably consider getting an advisor, Mr. Jacobs, someone with intimate knowledge of the inner workings of the Intelligence community and the ability to keep abreast of current ops." She gave him a dazzling smile.

"You wouldn't happen to have a business card would you, Mr. Jacobs?"

Brad stared at her. “Really? I’ve never even thought about having business cards printed up.”

“Well, I’m not suggesting you pass them around like an insurance salesman, Mr. Jacobs, but it seems to me that you’ve made a real name for yourself and you really should be able to present a business card to a legitimate prospect seeking your services. Something to keep in mind.” She turned away to leave.

“I didn’t catch your name Mrs…”

She turned to face him again. “I didn’t offer it, and it’s Ms…” Just as she was about to leave, she turned again. “I’m going to send a friend to you, Mr. Jacobs. I think you and your team are exactly what he needs to solve a rather ticklish problem in the Southern Cone. I understand that money is no object.” Then she was gone before he could even offer to tell her how to get in touch with him.

“Who was that?” Vicky was back, reaching for his champagne flute. “She looked vaguely familiar.”

“I have no idea. She said she just retired from the Intelligence community in D.C. but she didn’t say with who… She asked me for a business card and then she said she was going to send someone to see us. Something about the Southern Cone and money being no object. She seemed to know a lot about Team Dallas. She said we had come pretty close to stepping on some very important toes in D.C.”

“That’s not surprising,” Vicky murmured. “She didn’t even give you a clue as to which agency she might have been working for?”

“Not a hint. Whoever she was working for, she had access to classified State Department files.” Brad turned to look in the direction the tiny woman had gone, but there was no longer any sign of her. She had faded into the crowd like a pro. “I don’t know, maybe Charlie might have some idea.”

Charlie Dawkins, a former State Department Special Agent in their little-known enforcement arm, still had some connections to the Intelligence community. Charlie had joined Team Dallas because of his relationship with Brad's gorgeous cousin Jessica, a former treasure hunter and adventuress who had proven herself a tremendous asset to Team Dallas on her own merit.

Brad turned back to Vicky. "Do you think she was right? Should I actually have a business card?"

"I keep telling you darling," Vicky said, giving him a squeeze, "you do this because it is who you are, not because it's what you do for a living, but it's still a business and you are going to have to start treating it like one."

"I'm not going to deny that I like having the money, baby, but it seems kind of, I don't know ... wrong to treat it as a business. I do this because I believe it's the right thing to do."

"And that's a big part of why I feel the way I do about you, Brad, but if you don't think of anything else, just think about how much better you're going to be able to do your missions with the advanced equipment and weapons you can afford now. There's a lot of stuff out there that can make these missions safer for your team and for your clients. Treat it as a business, Brad. Let's get better at what we do." She gave him a peck on the cheek, drawing more envious stares from the cattlemen and even a few from their ladies. "And, yes, I think you need a business card."

FOUR

Day 0, San Benito, San Salvador, El Salvador

Ernesto Cruz was scared. Death was nothing new to him, the gangs in San Salvador had seen to that. The country of El Salvador had turned into a playground for the street gangs that had proliferated after the civil war. It was true that the gangs' ranks had been augmented by El Salvadorian youths who had been deported from cities in the U.S., but the new gang members didn't make them more vicious than before, their Mayan heritage and culture had taken care of that. What the new blood brought with them from the States was more modern technology and a broader spectrum of targets. The new guys knew where the money was and how to get it. The lack of a strong central government and the spreading influence of the gangs had resulted in El Salvador being elevated to the unenviable rank of "Murder Capital of the World." Ernesto saw death in all its forms on a daily basis, a mind-numbing experience for an eleven-year-old boy.

The fear sprouted from a new terror. Up until this very day, wealthy foreigners, especially ones who brought new businesses (and with them, jobs) to El Salvador, had been strictly off-limits to the gangs. The PNC had been very diligent in protecting those individuals and so had the private security forces, but this atrocity had not been committed by the gangs, it had been perpetrated by the men of El Caiman. The PNC and the private security forces had turned a blind eye to the whole thing ... and that was something new and horrifying.

Unsure of what he should do, Ernesto ran to the one person he was absolutely certain he could trust, the priest in his own village, a tiny farm community north of Tonacatepeque, a short distance north of Soyapango. Father Pietro was a young, bearded man on his first assignment to his own church and a great admirer of Saint Óscar Romero y Galdámez, former archbishop of San Salvador. The revered saint had been outspoken against poverty, social injustice, assassinations, and torture. In 1980, he had been assassinated while celebrating mass in the chapel of the Hospital of Divine Providence.

Ernesto ran the whole way to the little chapel in the darkness, sticking to the fields and orchards once he left the city. When he reached the stone chapel, he was sobbing, and he pounded on the doors of the sanctuary with his fists until they were bruised and swollen before the priest could dress and come to the door.

"Ernesto, my child! Why have you come to me at this hour? What is wrong with you?" Father Pietro was very devout, and he did not like to be interrupted during his evening prayers. Even so, the anguish and fear on Ernesto's little face were real and the young priest genuinely cared for his parishioners.

Gasping for breath, Ernesto blurted out what he had seen in agonizing detail. Father Pietro, uncertain as to whether the boy was recounting an actual event or an imagined terror, took the child inside to the small apartment added onto the rear of the chapel for the use of the parish priest and sat him down at the small table.

Knowing Ernesto's fondness for *champurrado* (hot chocolate thickened with corn flour), Father Pietro poured milk into a small pan and placed it onto one of the burners of his tiny gas stove to heat. "Breathe, Ernesto. Rest a moment while I make you a cup of champurrado and then tell me again what you have seen."

When the drink was almost boiling, Father Pietro poured the sweet drink into a handle less cup, which the boy accepted gratefully with both small hands. The priest pulled a chair close and sat down to listen.

"It's true, Padre, every word. El Caiman's men came to Senor Feng's house with guns, lots of guns!" Ernesto blew softly into the cup to cool the beverage slightly before he took a calming sip. "They took Senorita Meng and Senorita Chu Hua and marched them down the street like animals." Ernesto's eyes, still swollen from his earlier tears, burst into tears again. "They shot Humberto, Padre! Right in the face while he was standing in the big house next to Senor Feng!"

"It's over now, Ernesto. Tell me again about the men. Are you sure they were El Caiman's men?"

"Si Padre, I am sure. They were dressed all in black and they had El Caiman's sign on their sleeves. I am sure."

Father Pietro sat back in the rickety wooden chair, seething with anger. The fact that a man like El

Caiman could do anything he pleased without fear of punishment from the PNC or the government of El Salvador infuriated him. When he had asked the bishop if anything could be done about the man, the bishop had counselled him to be patient.

"We can only do what we can do, my son. We must try to remember that God works in mysterious ways and that even evil has a purpose in this world. Temporal matters are not for us to resolve. Tend to your flock and leave these things to others. We already have more obligations than we can handle."

The young priest was angered by what he perceived to be the uncaring attitude of the Church hierarchy toward the plight of the people of El Salvador, and he was incensed by the inaction of the government. Someone had to stand up for his parishioners, no matter what the cost.

* * *

The Command Center was a concrete reinforced strong room in the bowels of the thirty-eight-room mansion El Caiman had invaded and stolen from a hapless Columbian drug lord. The drug lord had kept his money and valuables in the strong room, but El Caiman had put it to better use. The inside walls of the room were lined with the most sophisticated electronic security and surveillance systems available on the commercial market. The center was manned twenty-four hours a day and the control operator inside was in constant contact with the perimeter guards and the interior guards.

El Caiman spent a great deal of his time in the office inside the Command Center because of the well-equipped communications desk he maintained there. His business ventures extended far beyond the borders of El Salvador, though few of his employees were aware of it and none of them knew the full extent, only he knew the whole picture. His empire was structured so that the whole thing would collapse without him. His office was also the place where he issued marching orders to his number two.

* * *

El Caiman read the flyer over for the third time and then glanced up at Piccard. "The priest was passing these out? Why? Half the villagers can't even read their own language!"

"He's not just passing them out. He's reading them aloud, in public. I'm told he even denounced you from his pulpit Sunday morning. He's making a real commotion over the Feng snatch too."

"Damned nuisance priests! They have far too much influence over these ignorant people!" El Caiman groused. "I can't let this pass, Lucien. Apparently these people are just like the cartels, they have to get a harsh reminder that my patience has limits now and again." He looked at his number two man. "You say the priest is in Tonacatepeque?"

"No sir, a little village, a hamlet really, just northwest of Tonacatepeque. So small it doesn't even have a name. The priest does have some influence in Tonacatepeque though. Word is out that he intends to do a little street corner preaching in the bigger town this weekend."

"We can't have him spouting off about our operations, Lucien. It's bad for business and it encourages the peasants to resent us ... and then resist us. I've worked too hard and too long setting this up to let some religious fanatic stir up the locals against me. If the people stop being afraid of me, the government will have to step in again ... and you know what a hard time the PNC gave us when we first took up operations here. It cost me a lot of men and money to settle them last time, and I don't want to have to go through that again." The large man shook his head then looked away from Piccard and sighed.

"Take the Strike Team, Lucien. You know what needs to be done."

Lucien knew El Caiman didn't like to be bothered with unnecessary talk; he spun on his heel and headed for the door. When his hand touched the doorknob, El Caiman spoke again.

"And Lucien, make it convincing, understand? Like in Mali."

Piccard understood. He was to make an example of the priest and then leave just enough people alive so they could spread the word about what might happen if they crossed El Caiman. He felt the same addictive mix of excitement and revulsion at what he was about to do in the little hamlet north of Tonacatepeque.

* * *

The rehearsal was a bit of overkill, but Piccard was a highly trained professional. The core cadre of El

Caiman's small army was staffed by former legionnaires, men he had served with or who had served under other men he trusted in the Legion. The staffers, as subordinate leaders, supervised and led the outsiders, predominantly mercenaries, castoffs from regular military units around the world. The hardest thing about controlling the mercs was restraining them in this particular type of operation. They were brutal men, and they had brutal tastes. Piccard knew that the killing instilled fear in the locals, but he also knew that ravishment and rape instilled anger and resentment more than it did fear. Many of the mercs did not understand that, and they were hard to control in this type of combat. Privately, Piccard had given very strict orders to the core cadre. Men caught in the act of rape were to be terminated with extreme prejudice, and the less said about it the better.

As the subordinate leaders went through the almost ritual inspections and rehearsals, Piccard was deep in thought. The youngest captive, Chu

Hua, had enchanted him more than he would have believed possible. It was rare for him to have anything on his mind other than his day-to-day business. There hadn't been a woman in his life other than the street whores in San Salvador in several years; now, all of a sudden, his head was filled with images of the firm, pale young flesh of Chu Hua, and the intoxicating scent she wore haunted him. The image of her, long, silky black hair, her pale skin, her sloe eyes, and the delicate features of her face remained in front of his eyes even though he hadn't seen her since he'd brought the two young women back to El Caiman's stronghold. Obsession was a new emotion for Piccard, and he didn't yet recognize it for what it was.

"Lucien!"

Piccard's head snapped around to see El Caiman standing in the doorway of the ops shed in full battle gear. "Yes sir?"

"I changed my mind. I think it is important that the people see me in person this time. I will be leading the operation, and, besides, I want to see this priest with my own eyes."

"Yes sir!" Piccard thought it was a ridiculous idea, but he had learned to keep his own counsel around El Caiman over the years. The man was not overly fond of his subordinates disagreeing with him, and doing so was risking serious consequences. El Caiman could be mercurial at the best of times.

* * *

There were no black balaclavas, no face scarves, no attempt whatsoever to hide the identities of the men. El Caiman himself led the column into the village, and his was the first unsuppressed weapon to begin chattering when they entered the small square. With a roar he unleashed his men, who fired indiscriminately into the village and tossed their fragmentation grenades into the modest homes of the villagers. It was ugly, and it was short, and it was devastating.

El Caiman stopped the massacre when Father Pietro was dragged before him in the square and cast down on the rough cobblestones. The villagers that were left, sobbing and wailing, were herded into the square and forced to watch.

Father Pietro managed to maintain his dignity and tried to struggle to his feet, but his captors forced him to remain on his knees in front of the warlord. His mouth was dry from fear, but he managed to work up enough saliva to spit.

"I thought I knew Satan," he said slowly. "They spoke of him often at the seminary. Now I know for certain that what they told me was wrong. Satan isn't in Hell..." His voice grew stronger, his back erect, and a look of sheer rebellion washed over his bruised and battered face. "Satan is before you! Look on his countenance! This man is the very definition of evil, my children. Do not fear him, he can only take your earthly—" Those were the last words he ever said. El Caiman executed him at that moment, silencing the brave priest forever. Then he turned to the villagers that remained, and he laughed.

* * *

El Caiman studied the faces of the two captives. Neither one was really his type, but he had noticed that Piccard seemed unusually interested in the younger one and for some reason that really annoyed him. He was more than a little paranoid, always watching for any sign of disloyalty. Even an imagined slight was cause for caution as far as he was concerned. Piccard was an old comrade in arms, but even he was not above suspicion. It wouldn't hurt to put him to a little test...

"I think the older one can be put into the pipeline right away, Lucien. Take care of that for me, would you?"

"Yes sir, I'll do that right away." Piccard was struggling with himself, not wanting to ask a question but unable to stop himself. "The younger one, sir..."

"Chu Hua, Lucien, her name is Chu Hua. Yes, what about Chu Hua?" This was intriguing. Piccard was usually as stolid a man as El Caiman had ever known, but something about this slip of a girl had him nonplussed. He decided to scratch the scab over whatever this was about.

"What ... what do you want me to do with her?"

"Take her to one of the spare bedrooms and lock her inside, Lucien. Leave one of the interior security men to guard the room, I may decide to sample this one myself before putting her in the pipeline." He smiled, a knowing, lecherous smile put on just to agitate Lucien further. He had no intention of even touching this half-woman, she was not to his taste at all, but Lucien didn't know that.

"Yes sir."

Piccard's face, despite his efforts to hide it, showed his dismay, and El Caiman was even more intrigued. Dissension in the palace guard? It was not unheard of, and Piccard would not be the first good man to be corrupted by a bit of fluff. The man would bear watching.

* * *

Piccard was utterly unfazed by El Caiman's ruthlessness in the little village, but as he led the sobbing Chu Hua up to one of the guest rooms upstairs, near El Caiman's suite, he found himself deeply sympathetic towards her. As he thought of El Caiman's rough, hairy hands on her creamy flesh, his emotions went well past sympathy and kicked into actual anger. He had to do something to protect her!

For the first time since he'd know the man, Piccard had a disloyal thought. He needed to make sure

Chu Hua remained unsullied by his boss … even if it meant he had to do something drastic. He wanted Chu Hua for himself.

FIVE

Day 0, The Manor House, 1300 hours

The shiny black stretch limousine with dark tinted windows turned into a long driveway lined with large cottonwood trees that had been planted at least seventy years ago. The driveway meandered through a rolling forty-acre pasture and up to a white two-story Victorian home with a wraparound porch. The trim was painted a glossy dark green, and there were a couple of wooden swings painted the same color suspended on chains from the ceiling on the porch. Behind the house was a six-car garage, an enormous barn, a stable, a carriage house, a long, low bunkhouse, and a collection of outbuildings of various sizes, all painted to match the main house.

The limousine stopped at the apex of the circular drive in front of the house, and a Chinese gentleman wearing an impeccably tailored black suit and thick, black glasses stepped out of the backseat carrying a slim briefcase; he marched across the brick pavers up to the front door.

Vicky answered the door dressed in jeans and a western shirt, her red hair tied back with a bandana.

"Is this the residence of Mr. Brad Jacobs?" The man seemed skeptical, and Vicky's first impression was that the guy was some kind of high dollar salesman, the kind that shows up in droves when they get a whiff of new money in their territory. Vicky adjusted her stance unnoticeably to a defensive position, prepared to shut the door at the first sign of aggressive behavior.

"Depends on who's asking," Vicky said suspiciously.

The visitor recognized the subtle shift in her stance for what it was and his demeanor instantly changed.

"I apologize," he said, producing a business card from the breast pocket of his coat. "I am Wu Li Jun, Security Adviser for Feng Industries, and I am here to discuss a matter of grave import with Mr. Jacobs."

"Is he expecting you?" Vicky inwardly cursed herself, knowing she had slipped up, letting the man know that Brad was, in fact, at home.

"In a manner of speaking, yes. At least, he was advised by a mutual acquaintance that I would be coming. I am sorry to intrude, but it really is imperative that I speak with Mr. Jacobs as soon as possible. There are lives at stake."

Vicky appraised the man quickly. He was not carrying a weapon unless he had it in the slim briefcase, and he wasn't standing the way an armed man would. She, of course, was carrying a weapon concealed in a holster at the small of her back. The driver of the limo remained inside the vehicle.

"Very well then, Mr. Wu, please, come inside and make yourself comfortable while I go to tell Brad you are here." She led him into the vaulted foyer and then off into the formal living room with its comfortable leather sofa and chairs. "Have a seat, I will just be a moment." She turned and walked down the hall to Brad's study, which was still filled with boxes and cartons from his old study.

Brad was sitting in an overstuffed chair, sipping coffee and staring at a wad of power cords and USB cables in the corner. "I'm never going to get all this crap sorted out, Vicky, you know that, right?"

Vicky waved a hand at the pile dismissively. "You don't need to have it in the house at all, Brad. I thought we were going to build you an office in the barn anyway."

Brad sighed. "I know. Force of habit I guess. I'm still kind of overwhelmed by all this. Duckworth really threw me a curve ball with this place. I have no idea what I'm going to do with all this."

Vicky leaned over and hugged him. "Face it, baby, you're officially in the big time now. Trust your own judgment. You know what you need to do, you just haven't applied that military mind of yours to an assessment of what you have and what you need. You will figure it out in no time!" She kissed his forehead and then straightened up.

"Right now, however, you have a visitor." She held out her hand. "Come on, he says lives are at stake."

* * *

"It's good to meet you, Mr. Jacobs. I've heard a great deal about you recently, and I'm told you are the best in the business." The man's handshake was firm and dry.

"I'm sorry, Mr. Wu, you have me at a disadvantage. What business are we talking about?"

"Why, the business of killing, Mr. Jacobs." The Chinese beamed at him.

Brad stood up, his face tight. "I'm sorry, Mr. Wu, you've been misinformed. I'm not in the business of killing. I'm in the business of rescuing people held hostage, in situations where it is impossible for our government to intervene for one reason or another. Killing is something that is sometimes a necessary adjunct to my missions, but it is never my primary purpose. Vicky can show you to the door." He turned to leave, his temper flaring and rushing toward the surface.

"Wait, Mr. Jacobs! Please. Perhaps I stated it incorrectly. There are lives at stake, two young girls. They were abducted from their home in San Salvador three days ago."

Brad stopped and turned back to Wu. "All right, you've got my attention. Why hasn't the government done something? I know they have cops in El Salvador."

"PNC," Vicky interjected, "the Policia Nacional Civil."

"The PNC then, can't they do anything?" He glanced questioningly at Vicky.

"The PNC's hands are tied," Wu said.

"The PNC's hands are bought," Vicky corrected.

"They are not all paid off. The threat they face from the gangs is bad enough, but this man has them so intimidated that they not only ignore his activities, they provide security for his headquarters ... more to protect the citizens from El Caiman than the other way around."

"Who is this guy?"

"No one seems to know his real name, Mr. Jacobs. He came to El Salvador several years ago and started out as a transportista, a courier, or mule. He has a cadre of highly trained men, military types, and they are ruthless. No one is safe from them, not the government, the NPC, even the gangs and cartels are afraid of him. He is untouchable."

"The cartels are afraid of him?" Brad asked, incredulous.

Wu nodded. "Very much so. When El Caiman decided to expand his business, he and his men assaulted and took over a cartel hardsite, a fortress if you will. It belonged to the Columbians. They tried to take it back, but they could not. Afterwards, El Caiman set his men to disrupting the cartel's shipments, attacking and killing the Columbians and anyone who worked for them. Over a period of six bloody months, there was a war, one that saw many people killed—PNC, military, cartel, gangs, and civilians. Eventually there was a truce. Then it was business as usual, except that none of them trifled with El Caiman any longer. He became untouchable."

"Jesus! How come I never heard of this guy?"

"I've heard rumors," Vicky said. "Nothing concrete, but then I was focused on child trafficking."

"That has not been the main thrust of his business, but it has become more prevalent in recent months. El Caiman has discovered that there is a huge profit from a resource that costs him little or nothing. It has become a real problem and it is the reason I am here. The girls are the daughters of Feng Jingguo, president and CEO of Feng Industries. As you may know, relations between China and the U.S. are a bit strained at the moment ... negotiations over tariffs and international trade. Because of the uncertainty, China has encouraged businesses to expand their footprints beyond her borders. El Salvador is one of the nations targeted because of inexpensive land, lower labor costs, and highly favorable tax breaks."

"He means cheap labor honey," Vicky said tightly. She was not overly fond of what she considered exploitation of indigenous workers in underdeveloped nations.

Wu gave her a mildly annoyed look before continuing. "Feng Industries is an appliance manufacturer, and it employs several thousand workers who had no jobs at all before it opened its doors. Many of them had never had a regular job before. Company-provided training, continuing education, healthcare, and daycare are rarities in El Salvador, but Feng Industries provides them for its workers. It is true the workers are paid less than their equivalents in the U.S., but their salaries are more than double the average income of their peers in El Salvador." He was plainly miffed at Vicky's comment, but he quickly recovered and resumed his pitch.

"El Caiman's men came to Mr. Feng's residence and abducted his two daughters, Meng and Chu Hua." Wu removed two eight-by-ten photographs and passed them to Brad. "They executed Mr. Feng's butler in the foyer, in front of the girls and Mr. Feng. These men are very bad, Mr. Jacobs, merciless."

Brad studied the two images and then passed them to Vicky. "When did this happen?"

"Four days ago. We have heard nothing from El Caiman or his men since. We have no idea if the girls are alive or dead."

"Jesus Wu!" Brad exclaimed, standing upright suddenly, his balled up fists revealing the extent of his agitation. "You're a security adviser! You should know that the first forty-eight hours are critical!" Brad paced around the living room, frowning in frustrated concentration.

"No ransom demand?"

"Not a word."

"You realize that those kids are probably already dead or on their way to some pervert in the Middle East or Africa now, right?"

Wu was unruffled. "Mr. Jacobs, I'm Chinese. I daresay we have more experience with this sort of thing than any other culture on Earth. After all, we have five thousand years of recorded history behind us. There is no refinement of any form of evil that we have not seen."

"Then, dammit, you should know that finding and rescuing those two girls is damned near impossible! Too much time has passed."

"We are well aware of that likelihood, Mr. Jacobs. That is why Mr. Feng has sent me here. He wishes you to kill El Caiman and stop the evil."

Brad stopped midstride. "I told you before, I am not some kind of hit man..."

"Mr. Jacobs, please, just think of this as an exercise in semantics. Mr. Feng is willing to pay handsomely for you to go into El Salvador and try to locate his two daughters. If you should happen to run into El Caiman in the process, and you most surely will, he will try to kill you. It will purely be a matter of self-defense." Wu reached into the expensive leather briefcase once more and came out with a large thumb drive, proffering it to Brad. "Please, Mr. Jacobs, watch this before you answer me."

Brad's temper was about to snap when Vicky stepped forward and took the thumb drive from Wu's hand. "We will see what's on this drive, Mr. Wu, but I assure you Mr. Jacobs is not a 'hit man'."

"That is all I could ask, Ms. Chance, thank you."

"How can we get in touch with you when we are through watching this?"

"That will not be a problem, Ms. Chance. I shall wait in the limousine. I must make several urgent calls and that should provide you sufficient time to view the files on the drive. I can see myself out."

Brad and Vicky watched, astonished, as Wu made his way unerringly back to the front door as if he was as familiar with the house as he was with his own.

"How the hell did he do that?" Brad fumed.

"How the hell did he know my name?" Vicky mused. "I never introduced myself." They stared at each other and then at the thumb drive in Vicky's hand.

"Arrogant sonofabitch!"

"Easy Brad. We're talking about two kids here. Let's read the files before we jump to conclusions."

"Vicky, those girls are most probably dead, or worse, by now, you know that. Jesus! Four days!"

"I know no such thing, Brad, and neither do you! We need to look at the evidence on this drive and then do a little research of our own before we form an opinion."

"Wu's going to be waiting out in that limo..."

"Screw the arrogant sonofabitch." Vicky smiled. "Let him wait." She palmed the thumb drive and led the way back to Brad's study, her slender hips swaying fetchingly.

* * *

Brad sat down at the battered old roll top desk the movers had brought from the study at his old place and booted up the slim laptop he had used for years.

"That thing looks kind of ratty, Brad. I think it's time to upgrade some of our electronics now, that thing is kind of embarrassing."

"It's done what I needed it to for years, baby, and, besides, I know how to use it."

"You don't apply that same rationale to your weapons, Brad, why would you apply it to your computer? Haven't you pounded your philosophy into my head over and over? 'Everything is a weapon! When given a choice, go for the best!' You should take your own advice."

She leaned forward and plugged the thumb drive into a USB port on the side of the laptop and sat down beside him to watch as Brad accessed the "D" drive and opened the first video file.

They watched together as the video opened on the screen. Both of them had seen sights in their lifetimes that no human should ever have to see, but neither was prepared for the stark gruesomeness of the scene unfolding before them.

The video had no commentary, it was just a silent record of carnage that reminded Brad strongly of the Allied films made in World War II. The video was apocalyptic, showing what was clearly some Central American village in ruins. Smoke from recently burned buildings drifted through the air onscreen, and there was a close-up of bullet-riddled walls. Then came the bodies, lying in clumps on the unpaved streets, hanging out of windows and lying in doorways. It was more than

Vicky could bear to watch, and she turned her head away.

Brad, his face a grim mask of determination, forced himself to watch. Military casualties he had seen in war, but these were civilians ... and no one had been spared as far as he could see. The killing seemed indiscriminate, with no age group or sex excluded. There were even domestic animals included in the slaughter.

"Shit!" he breathed when the video concluded. But there was more to follow—redacted reports, written on official U.S. government stationery (with the agency logos redacted as well), screen prints of blogs and scanned pages from personal journals decrying atrocity after atrocity. All of it was attributed to the men in black wearing El Caiman's logo on their sleeves. There were more videos, some taken from places of hiding, of the killings, the torture, and the hangings.

"Jesus Vicky! Who is this guy? Hell, even the Taliban had more mercy than he does!" Up until he had seen the contents of the thumb drive, he had considered the Afghans the most ruthless people he had ever seen or heard of, but the actions of this "Caiman" character and his henchmen far exceeded the sheer cruelty of the Afghans.

"I don't know," she said between gritted teeth, "but I'm sure as hell going to find out. Someone is turning a blind eye to this crap and I don't like it one damned bit!" There were tears in her eyes, very out of character for her.

* * *

"I don't know who this bastard is paying off, Brad, but it's somebody with a lot of juice in government. All of my contacts in the Intelligence community so far have heard of El Caiman, but nobody seems to know—or will admit to knowing—who he really is."

"That doesn't make any sense!" Brad shook his head. "How in the hell does he get away with this crap without anybody catching on to him, Vicky?" The thumb drive had contained more than an hour of videos and documentation from official (heavily redacted) and reliable unofficial sources. "I don't even recall seeing any of this in the media."

"Like I said, he apparently has some serious influence, and obviously some very deep pockets. That kind of pull doesn't come cheap."

Brad's face wore an angry scowl. "This is unbelievable, Vicky, but in spite of what I've seen here, I'm not going to send Team Dallas down there on a hit job. I'll pack it in first!"

"I agree with you, Brad, but there's no way we can let this go without doing something about it. Nobody should have to live like those people are—nobody... And those kids!" Angry tears flowed down her cheeks as she stared unblinking at some of the most horrific images either of them had ever seen.

“Not to mention these two girls,” Brad spat. He tossed the two photographs onto the top of his desk.

Vicky swung around to face him. “You realize that anything we do is probably going to be too late for them, don’t you?”

“Yeah,” Brad growled, “but maybe El Caiman will get stupid and fire on us. I’d rather bust his ass and drop him off at a C.I.A. or State Department field office, but it won’t break my heart if he doesn’t survive the rescue effort.”

“So we’re going to take the contract?”

“Not a contract hit, Vicky. I’m not willing to take the job on those terms.”

“That’s all he’s offered… What’s going on in that devious head of yours, Brad?”

Brad frowned again. “I’m more than a little pissed that they waited so long to contact us. What kind of father would hold off for this long and then try to put out a hit on the guy responsible instead of calling in the cavalry to go get them as soon as it happened?”

“You ever been to Hong Kong, Brad?”

“I landed at Kai-Tak Airport once, but I never got off the plane.”

“In Aberdeen Harbor there is a floating village of junks, all tied together. Years ago, when I first visited there, I saw people who had lived all their lives on those boats without their feet ever touching land. They were called the Haklo or Tanka people.”

“That’s fascinating,” Brad said drily, “but what has that got to do with Feng’s daughters?”

“The Haklo tied ropes around their infant sons so that they didn’t fall off the junks into the harbor—

which smells to high heaven, by the way—and drown. They didn't bother with the infant girls. They didn't care about the girls; they referred to them as 'little useless mouths.'"

"Jesus! How long ago was this?"

"I was just a kid then, Brad, but I've never forgotten that. I'm not saying that Feng treats his daughters that way, but it's something to keep in the back of your mind. The Chinese see things differently than we do. It's weird, though, because even though the Haklo were so unfeeling about their daughters, the Chinese as a whole believe that family is the most important thing on Earth ... after money."

Brad pursed his lips and frowned again. "So this is all about vengeance and not about the daughters?"

"I would say more about the vengeance than about the girls, but we really can't make that assumption, Brad. We don't know this guy and my contacts don't know any more about Feng than they do about El Caiman."

"Do you think there is the remotest chance those kids are still alive?"

"I think we have to consider that El Caiman is probably in the human trafficking business like Wu said, and that means they are probably still alive. Neither of those girls is ugly, and there is a very big market for young women, regardless of their ethnic backgrounds. Traffickers rarely kill their own profits. Occasionally they kill one of the more recalcitrant girls as an example to the other abductees, but that's really pretty rare. Those kids are already terrified, and you can't blame them."

"Then we operate on the assumption that they are still alive. Do we have any ideas about his 'pipeline', where it originates, transfer points, destinations, stuff like that?"

"All we have is the point of origin," Vicky said. The tip of her index finger was pointing at a spot on the map open on Brad's laptop marked as El Caiman's compound. "We'll have to start there and try to trace his 'pipeline'. Maybe we'll get lucky and the girls will still be there."

And maybe we'll get luckier still and the bastard will try to keep us from freeing them so we can kill him, she thought. Vicky kept that thought to herself.

SIX

Day 0, The Manor House, 1721 hours

Wu settled into the expensive soft leather armchair in the living room, facing Brad. He did not appear unsettled in the least, despite having spent the better part of three hours in the back of the limousine.

"Have you come to a decision, Mr. Jacobs?" There were none of the inconsequential pleasantries Brad had come to expect from the Oriental businessmen he had dealt with in the past. Chinese or not, this guy had been educated in the U.S. and had adopted some of the less pleasant U.S. business practices. Brad knew a shark when he saw one.

"Brad, would you and your guest like a cup of coffee?" Willona called from the kitchen.

"I didn't know she was here," Brad muttered under his breath.

"I'll take care of it, Brad," Vicky said.

"Tell her I'd prefer something stronger, please. That little show left a bad taste in my mouth." He turned to Wu. "What about you? Too early for a drink?"

Wu was caught off guard. "No, I, uh, coffee for me, please. I don't drink while I'm working. Mr. Feng doesn't approve."

Brad grunted and checked his watch. It was well after five o'clock. Wu wasn't as Americanized as he'd thought.

"I have a counterproposal, Mr. Wu," he said pleasantly.

Wu leaned forward in the chair, gripping his briefcase tightly in both hands. "I can listen, and I can relay your counterproposal to Mr. Feng, but I can tell you he is adamant. He insists on a final solution to El Caiman."

"As I told you earlier, Mr. Wu, I don't run a team of assassins. After the evidence you've shown me, there is not a doubt in my mind that the world would be a better place without this El Caiman in it. That being said, I am not a murderer. Yes, my team and I have killed but only in combat. The United States is not at war with El Salvador."

"Of course," Vicky interjected, "there is the possibility—maybe even the probability—that El Caiman will put up a fight when we come to take the girls back. That could easily prove to be fatal." Brad gave her a sour look.

Wu thought for a moment. "Mr. Jacobs, you and your team have killed in a number of incidents—missions I believe you call them—in places where the U.S. is not at war. Besides, I am given to understand that as a sniper, in combat, several members of your team have performed missions where terrorist leaders or political figures met the technical definition of an assassination. You and Mr., ah, Smoot come to mind."

"I'm not going to debate the issue with you, Mr. Wu. What I did, under lawful orders from the officers appointed above me as a Marine, have no bearing on the missions I accept for Team Dallas. The missions we have undertaken since my separation from the Corps are a different matter entirely. We kill in self-defense or in defense of our clients. I repeat, we are not assassins."

Wu remained unperturbed. "El Caiman is using these kidnappings—Mr. Feng's daughters are not the first, by the way—to take control over new businesses coming into El Salvador. He has a much larger plan than just taking over Feng Industries. These companies will be the salvation of thousands of penniless families and a major boost to the economy of El Salvador."

"I don't understand why the government hasn't taken care of this lunatic themselves. This would seem to me like an issue for them to deal with."

"The government is weak, Mr. Jacobs," Wu said patiently. "They have been unable to handle the gangs and the cartels, both of which are intimidated to the point of helplessness by El Caiman. The governments of other countries have their hands tied by the delicacy of ongoing trade and tariff negotiations. For all of them, including your own, this is what you might call a Catch-22. Feng Industries is a government sponsored entity of China's, and they are very seriously concerned that El Caiman is going to present what they coyly referred to as 'difficulties' when I met with their representatives unless a satisfactory, and permanent, solution is effected."

Vicky returned, carrying a tray bearing a steaming mug of coffee, cream, sugar, and a tumbler containing three fingers of Russell's Reserve Rye whiskey. She served the coffee to Wu first then handed the tumbler to Brad, who took a healthy swallow before setting it down on a side table.

"To that end," Wu continued, setting his coffee down and reaching for his briefcase, "I have been instructed by Mr. Feng and the government of China to offer you this retainer for your services." He reached into the briefcase and withdrew a legal-sized white envelope and handed it to Brad.

Vicky walked over behind Brad's chair, looking over his shoulder as he slit the envelope open with his thumbnail and extracted a check from inside. She was unable to stop her involuntary gasp at the amount on the check.

Brad managed not to gasp but covered his surprise with a cough.

Vicky recovered first. "Mr. Wu, I hate to ask you to wait any longer, but Brad and I need to talk about this before we give you an answer."

Wu started to get up, but Vicky waved him back into his seat. "This won't take long, we'll just step outside for a moment and be right back in." She grabbed Brad's hand and firmly tugged him toward the foyer.

Once they were safely outside, Brad was the first to speak. "Vicky, I know this is a buttload of money, but we don't need it and I am still not going to take a contract hit job."

"Frankly, I don't have a problem with it, Brad. Wu is right. This guy is worse than pond scum, and his continued existence on this earth is offensive to me. You know as well as I do that some people just need killing. El Caiman, left unchecked, is a mortal threat to a whole hell of a bunch of downtrodden people who have no one at all left to protect them ... and he's trying to take over the businesses that can lift them up out of poverty. Hell, I already hated him for his trafficking in kids!"

"Vicky, I know how you feel about all this, but the only thing I really give a damn about is those two girls."

"So don't take it as a 'hit' mission, Brad, but take it. This isn't about the money, even if that retainer is extravagant. I want a chance at that bastard!"

"I'll make the counterproposal, Vicky, but only under my terms. We are not going down there on a hit, period."

"But we can take him out if he shoots at us, right? I mean, he could even be collateral damage if he gets in the way..."

"I didn't know you were so bloodthirsty, Vicky." He grinned at her.

"I'm not bloodthirsty, Brad, and you know it! I just hate that bastard for what he's done. Human traffickers are lower than whale shit and if it was up to me every damn one of them would be hung upside down and castrated with a dull butter knife."

Brad laughed and hugged her. "That doesn't sound bloodthirsty at all, baby," he said, tongue in cheek. "Come on, let's go talk to Wu."

They turned together and walked back inside what Brad was already laughingly referring to as the Manor House.

* * *

"You said you'd have to present my counterproposal to Mr. Feng before you could offer the contract, Mr. Wu." He handed the envelope containing the retainer check back to the surprised security adviser. "Let me tell you my conditions. First, we go on this mission to rescue those girls, that is our primary mission. Second, we capture El Caiman after we get the girls and take him out of the country and turn him over to an agency we can trust not to cut him loose or be intimidated by him or his men—"

"That would have to be somewhere out of Central America," Wu interjected quickly.

"That goes without saying. I'm actually thinking here in Dallas would be best. There are several field offices of various agencies that would love to get their hands on him and I can get him through customs without too much trouble ... as a prisoner."

"Anything else, Mr. Jacobs?"

"That's it."

"I will present your counter to Mr. Feng; it may take a while to get a response from him, he's a very busy man. In the meantime, you're going to be contacted by a local individual with what I am assured are some very impressive Intelligence Community credentials with some additional details I am sure you will find very interesting. By the way, once I get approval I will need your response within forty-eight hours or I will be forced to seek out someone else with the ability to complete the contract."

Brad looked surprised. "If someone else would take the contract as a hit, why would you even bother with me?"

"Your reputation, Mr. Jacobs. I have it on the highest authority that you are the best currently in the business ... and I am told you have never failed to complete a mission successfully." Wu handed Brad back the retainer check. "I already know you are trustworthy, Mr. Jacobs. Think of this as a vote of confidence." He turned and picked up his briefcase. "I can show myself out. Have a good day, and you will hear from me as soon as I get Mr. Feng's approval."

* * *

“I can’t believe he left this with us!”

“He’s hoping the money will influence you if Feng doesn’t approve your counter offer, Brad.”

“Then he doesn’t know me as well as he thinks he does.” Brad reached for the almost forgotten tumbler of rye and downed the rest of it.

“He was pretty smug,” Vicky agreed.

“Something about this bothers me, baby. It bothers me that he’s willing to wait so long before going after those girls. Every second they are in that bastard’s hands increases the likelihood that we will never find a trace of them.”

“Not to mention the horrible things that may be already happening to them, Brad. Traffickers are known for sampling their wares before selling them. Only the very young are sold as virgins.”

Brad shook his head sadly. “This stinks.”

"We can only do what we can do, Brad. Nobody hates that more than I do, but it is what it is."

"That doesn't mean I have to like it, baby. What the hell is he keeping from us? There has to be something more that he hasn't mentioned. That is a real shitload of money." They both stared at the retainer check Wu had left with them. There were seven figures in the pay column.

SEVEN

Day 0+1, The Manor House, 0945 hours

The beautiful young woman with the slender build of a swimmer with muscles and long blonde hair hanging down past the curve of her butt stood in the living room of what Brad was referring to as the Manor House with an air of satisfaction. Her name was Jessica Paul and she was Brad's cousin.

Jessica had been a treasure hunter, always looking to find a fortune that she could call her own instead of relying on the trust fund established for her by her father, Brad's Uncle Jack. She had gotten into a real bind in the Congo looking for diamonds, and Brad and his team had come to her rescue. In the battle that followed her rescue, and the mission to Alaska where Brad had gone to rescue Pete Sabrowski and Charlie Dawkins, Jessica's boyfriend, from a plane crash, Jessica had proven herself to be a cool, level-headed warrior under fire. She had been a member of Team Dallas ever since.

When Brad and Vicky had moved into the Manor House, Vicky had been delighted that Jessica was willing to help with the selection of drapes and furnishings for the place, and Willona Ving, Mason Ving's wife and the Chief Financial Officer for the newly formed Jacobs & Ving Security LLC, had been just as happy to add her considerable skills in decorating to the endeavor.

"I think the place looks fantastic even if I do say so myself," Jessica remarked, standing with her hands on her hips and surveying the room.

"You do have an eye for color," Willona said.

"Where's Vicky? She should see this now that it's finished. I want to know what she thinks."

"She's out in the barn with Brad and Ving. They're setting up the new Team Dallas office."

* * *

When Vicky had enlisted Jessica to aid her in furnishing the place, Brad and Ving had gone about figuring out how to utilize the rest of the buildings. The barn was massive, and Brad had appropriated a large area on the first floor front of the barn as office space. Rather than try to build the office himself, he planned on hiring a remodeling crew to come in and build it for him.

Vicky had suggested that Brad make the office larger than he'd first sketched it, telling him he needed to leave room for possible future expansion, and then she'd sketched in a bathroom, a kitchenette, and a conference room. "You guys eat like hogs, and Ving needs to be close to someplace where he can cook bacon to his heart's content," she'd quipped.

They had taped off the outlines of the outer walls based on the sketch and were discussing the inner layout over a Yellow Rose IPA beer when Jessica and Willona walked into the barn.

"You guys expecting company?" Jessica asked.

"No, why?"

"Because there's an old pickup truck coming up the driveway, Brad."

They all walked outside and watched the brown truck motor slowly up the winding drive lined with ancient cottonwoods until it came to a stop behind the shiny black Excursion parked by Vicky's Toyota. A tiny woman with long brown hair tied in a ponytail clambered down out of the cab and shut the door then tucked her thumbs in her back pockets and looked around at the house and outbuildings. Brad thought she looked vaguely familiar.

"This is a hell of a nice spread you've got here," she said. She turned and walked toward the four of them with her hand extended. "You probably don't remember me, we met at the Cattlemen's Association Ball. I'm Felicity Highsmith." Vicky remembered her, but she kept her mouth shut. Her curiosity was piqued.

"Okay, I remember you now," Brad said, taking her outstretched hand. "You're dressed a lot different today and the ponytail threw me. Come on in, we've just moved in here, but I'm sure we can offer you something cool to drink."

"Oh, I don't want to be a bother, Mr. Jacobs, I just stopped by to see where Jacobs & Ving were setting up shop ... or should I call it Team Dallas?"

Brad's eyebrows rose in surprise. "I'm a little surprised you know about that. The papers were only filed by our attorney a week or so ago, and we don't advertise."

"You and your team have quite a reputation in the Intelligence community Mr. Jacobs."

Brad's eyebrows rose even higher, and Vicky and Ving gave each other an inquisitive look.

"If that offer of something cool to drink is still good, I'll be happy to explain to you how I know about that," Felicity said with a coy smile.

They led her into the house after he introduced her all around and she shook hands with the others. Willona and Jessica went into the kitchen to get a pitcher of tea and glasses while Vicky led the way into Brad's study.

"This is where you plan your operations?" Felicity asked in disbelief, staring at Brad's antiquated (by current standards) laptop, his charts and maps, and the metal file cabinets. "From what I've heard of your exploits I would have expected you to be a little more high-tech."

"I'm sorry, Ms. Highsmith, but I'm a little curious as to how and why you seem to know so much about our business."

"Sorry, I guess I should explain myself. I retired from government service, in the Intelligence business, a little over a year ago. I am not only privy to a great deal of classified information, I designed and implemented a number of the systems that most of the agencies use."

Vicky's eyes widened and she pointed at their visitor. "I know who you are! Fly! You're that Highsmith … from NSA! You're kind of a legend over at MCIA (Marine Corps Intelligence Activity)."

"I wouldn't call myself a legend, but I did give it my best," Felicity said modestly.

"I always pictured you as a guy!" Vicky blurted.

Felicity laughed. "A lot of people make that mistake. No, I'm all girl."

"You specialized in the Southern Cone?"

"No, but that was an area of particular interest to me in the last years I was working, Ms. Chance."

"Please, call me Vicky."

"Then you can call me Fly. I used to hate that nickname, but I kind of miss it these days."

"You were asking about the technology we use Ms. ... Fly," Brad said. Clearly, Vicky knew this woman's reputation and respected her, and if she was retired from NSA she was damned sure likely to be familiar with the latest advancements in technology in the field. She would probably have some useful opinions about the equipment the team used. Vicky had been after him to upgrade his equipment...

"I guess I just sort of expected you to have a little more sophisticated setup based on your record of successes. I'm sorry, I didn't mean to be critical, and, after all, it's hard to argue with success..."

"Not at all. In fact, if you wouldn't mind, I'd like to show you the rest of our gear. It's still crated up out in one of the outbuildings, we haven't unpacked it since we moved it from our old warehouse."

"I'd be delighted!"

* * *

The outbuilding Brad referred to was a climate controlled concrete block building with a thick steel door. It was the most secure of the buildings on the property, and he had no idea what the former owner had used it for, but it was an almost ideal site for an arms room. What commo gear they had besides the secure Blackberries they all carried had been secured with the weapons and ammunition. He carried the odd looking key to the high security lock on his own keyring. The manufacturer had only included two keys with the expensive device, and Brad had been forced to go through some fairly extensive paperwork to special order copies for the other team members.

She had asked to see their commo equipment, but Brad and the others noticed she was paying as much attention to the assortment of weaponry as she was the electronics.

"Honestly, it's amazing to me how successful you've been with no more sophisticated communications equipment than you have, Brad. Even your own Force Recon is using Bluetooth two-way UHF technology with throat mikes and microcams. The commercial stuff is relatively cheap, about seventeen hundred bucks for a six-pack, but I know for a fact that you can get a boosted version that works on satellite instead of cellular towers, virtual real time communications with no lag, if you've got the cash..." She gave Brad a knowing look. "But then that's no longer a problem for you, is it?"

"If you've been retired for a year, how come you know so much about a mission we just finished?" Ving blurted out.

"You make a lot of useful contacts in the Intelligence business over time, Mr. Ving, and of necessity many of them are in industry, particularly industries whose international business interests might have a profound effect on matters of national security. One of the most vital, and therefore heavily scrutinized, of those is the oil industry. When I started out with NSA, one of my first contacts in that industry was an up-and-coming executive with Duckworth International Petroleum. His father was CEO and Chairman of the Board William Darnell Duckworth III." There was a moment of stunned silence, which Vicky was the first to break.

"So you've talked to Duckworth?"

"Bill and I have kept in touch over time, and, yes, we had a little chat just before the Cattlemen's Association Ball. " She changed tack quickly. "If you're not too busy at the moment, I'd like you to come over to my place. There have been some new technological developments, particularly in communications, that I think you might find extremely useful in your line of work."

"I never turn down a chance to improve my professional knowledge. You never know when the odd bit of knowledge might make the difference between finishing a mission or failure."

Vicky smiled at that. Brad's favorite saying was, 'Everything can be a weapon,' and he meant it literally.

* * *

Fly's ranch was less than twenty miles from the Manor House, and the five of them piled into the new Excursion for the short trip. She directed Brad to turn onto a graveled drive between two massive posts with an arched sign bearing the Lazy H brand suspended between them. The drive was far shorter than Brad and Vicky's, but it was lined with cedar elms instead of cottonwoods.

The ranch house was long and low, but Fly directed them to a large, white converted bunkhouse behind the main house. Atop the peak of the building was an array of small, sophisticated looking satellite dishes. A tall metal mast stabilized by guy wires stood at one end. Well up the narrow tower, perhaps halfway, was a bank of what appeared to be sets of transmitter/receivers, transceivers, digital signal processors, control electronics, and a GPS receiver. The setup looked, and was, very expensive.

“The guts are in here,” Fly said, pressing her eye to a laser optic recognition device and then inserting an even more hi-tech looking key than Brad’s into a recessed lock in a door that was far thicker and heavier than it first appeared.

The hum of computers and banks of equipment with varicolored blinking lights greeted the four of them as they entered the bunkhouse.

“Wow!” Ving exclaimed.

"I'll show you all this stuff later, guys, what I really brought you here to see is over in this corner," Fly said, leading them over to a long work table with direct overhead lighting.

"These," she said, picking up a couple of small, odd-shaped items from the top of the bench, "are called 'earwigs'." She handed one to Brad and one to Vicky. "With these you can actually receive signals in real time from satellite relays instead of from a cellular source. There is a control module that attaches to your belt." She lifted one of the modules from the table top and handed it to Brad. "On the outside of the module is a flat three-position switch that allows you to switch from cellular to satellite or both signals."

"We can talk through these?" Brad's face was a mask of disbelief.

"Of course not," Fly snorted. "You must be watching too much television! These are transceivers, probably the best in the world, but they can't transmit through the earwig. You hold them in your hands for a few minutes until they warm up then compress them. When you stick them in your ear, they will expand to fit to the contours of your ear canal.

"To transmit, you need one of these." She picked up a small device shaped like a dime, only thinner and far more flexible. "It fits on the hollow of your throat, like this." She demonstrated. With her hand she indicated that Brad should place the earwig into his ear, and he, Vicky, and Ving each grasped one of the earwigs and warmed it in their palms before placing them in their ears and then holding the matching control modules. Fly walked to the far end of the building and faced away from them.

"I'm whispering." Her voice came through the earwig clear and clean, with no sibilance or hissing. "This device can be muted by placing your index finger on the transmitter disc so that you don't cough or shout in your team's ears and deafen them. There is no lag, as you can tell for yourself. The control modules are set on satellite mode." She turned around and approached them.

"What's the range on these?"

"There is no maximum range, Brad. These things will work anywhere in the world as long as you are out in the open. They come in garbled if you're inside solid rock, and some alloys will block the transmissions, but normal wood and simple metals like tin or thin galvanized won't shield them."

"That's incredible," Vicky breathed.

"There's more. These units have GPS capability and the battery technology is some kind of lithium hybrid that is so classified the manufacturer won't even release it to NSA. These suckers will hold a charge for over twenty-four hours even under heavy operating loads ... and they're rechargeable to full capacity in under an hour with solar powered chargers."

The tactical potential of the devices was exploding in Brad's brain much like a claymore being detonated, leaving him speechless. Vicky and Ving had quickly grasped the significance of instant communications anywhere in the world on such tiny devices. Willona was the only one of them not entranced, she was thinking about the cost.

"Where in the hell can I buy some of these?"

"You can't, Mr. Jacobs. These are the only working models that have ever left the testing facility. That's one of the reasons I wanted you to come here."

"I don't understand."

"I came to see you today because Feng Jingguo is a sometime business associate of an old friend and contact of mine. He asked me for help and I thought of you right away, but I've been out of the loop for a year so I did a little checking to see what you've been up to lately. A lot of guys in your line of work tend to mysteriously disappear you know."

"Okay, so you're the contact Wu told me about?"

"Yes I am, and El Caiman is a person of interest to me. I have followed his exploits since he left the Foreign Legion, and, frankly, I hate his ass. Aside from the fact that I believe he is truly a threat, he is a vile and disgusting man with ambitions far bigger than taking over El Salvador. He is absolutely merciless and he will stop at nothing to get what he wants. I did everything I could to set the Intelligence community on him, but he has some powerful friends in D.C. and in the U.N. Nobody will touch him."

"He's a legionnaire?" Brad frowned.

"Who the hell is he?" Vicky asked. "Nobody seems to know much about him."

"They know, they're just afraid to talk about him. He has a long reach. The guy's name is Simon Leclerc, he's a native South African and he was convicted and imprisoned for crucifying villagers in Chad for entertainment ... not his first offense but it was the first time he got caught. The Legion gave him a summary court martial and sent him to La Santé Prison in Paris for life, but he escaped along with two of his cohorts from the Legion who were imprisoned with him."

"La Santé has a reputation for being a hell of a tough place to get out of," Ving remarked.

"A well-deserved reputation. The guards are armed, and they shoot first and ask questions later. Leclerc knew that, and when he broke out, he and Piccard and the other fellow killed a half dozen men and stole their weapons. The bastards actually waited for the pursuit and opened up on the first ones out of the gate. The Paris flics were called in to help, but Leclerc murdered the first ones on the scene just for kicks. They tell me that what followed was the biggest manhunt since they went after The Jackal, but Leclerc got away smooth. He had to have gotten help from somebody high up the food chain.

The Paris cops are not that impressive, but the *Police Nationale*, formerly the *Sûreté*, one of two national police forces, along with the *National Gendarmerie*, and the main civil law enforcement agency of France are no slackers and they put a blanket over the whole damned city. It was a bloodbath and they were humiliated. Nobody knows exactly how many of the national cops were killed. In typical French fashion, the whole incident was swept under the rug and never talked about again. They still don't respond to requests for details about Leclerc or the escape."

"Sounds like a real scumbag. Wu showed us some stuff on a thumb drive that really bothered me, and this fits right in with what we've seen."

"I gave Wu most of the footage on that thumb drive and all the documentation. He was just going to come talk to you and offer you the check. With Feng, everything is about money, he can't seem to comprehend that everything and everyone can't be bought and sold. What's happening in El Salvador is far too important to trust a mercenary to fix it." The look on Fly's face was deadly serious. "Leclerc has to be stopped, permanently. In his case, incorrigible is an absolute term. Nothing short of death is going to put a halt to that man's depravity. He's a true psychopath in every sense of the word."

"I think I understand how you feel about the man, but we just don't do contract hits. We go after criminals, sure, but we turn them in to the authorities when we catch them. I have no intention of turning either myself or my team members into criminals, Fly."

"So you're determined not to go to El Salvador?"

"I didn't say that. I said we aren't going to perform a contract hit. I've made a counter offer, even though I'm uncomfortable waiting so long to go after the girls. The chances of being able to track them down are diminishing by the minute."

"I know what you mean about the delay, Brad, but you need to know that Feng is not the one actually calling the shots. He can't do a thing until it is formally approved by his superiors in Beijing."

"He's working for the Chinese government?" Brad asked in surprise.

"Not exactly. Feng Industries is a government sponsored business, but the government calls the shots when it comes to matters of great importance or with political ramifications. His hands are effectively tied because of the delicacy of the ongoing tariff negotiations and trade agreement talks. China is looking hard for a way around the president's stand on the tariffs imposed by the Chinese on U.S. goods. He's talking about imposing equivalent taxes on their goods to make prices competitive and they are looking for a way to produce goods outside China in countries that currently don't have high tariffs on goods coming into the U.S. as a lot of other countries are involved in these negotiations at the moment and none of them want to be involved in a trade war."

"I think that's a chickenshit way to react to a damned crisis! I can't believe this president is putting up with all the pussyfooting."

"He's not, Brad. He doesn't even know about this. Washington is polarized right now. What one party wants the other party is dead set against. A lot of issues that need and deserve bipartisan support have been put on the back burner because of our outrageous political climate. In the meantime, the only people who have the balls to tell the president what is going on in El Salvador are being kept away from him at all costs. He just doesn't know."

"That's a load of horse crap!" Ving was furious. "Elected officials are supposed to work for us; they aren't up there to decide what the president knows or doesn't know. He's the leader for Pete's sake! He's the one who should be making the decisions, that's what he was elected to do."

Fly shook her head. "Washington has turned into La-La Land in the last forty or so years. Every politician on the Hill has their own agenda, and they all feel as if their causes take precedence over everything else. The media is buying into that mess as well. They're not interested in anything but ratings, and they're turning a blind eye to news that the American public has a right to hear. They're more interested in keeping the public abreast of the latest celebrity's rant of the week and keeping real issues understated, buried on page three, or out of the public eye altogether. In exchange for doing so, individual members of the Fourth Estate are rewarded with perks at the White House, parking spots at various government buildings, and access to the president while the mavericks are shunted to one side and ignored."

"It seems to have gotten worse since I left the Corps," Vicky muttered.

"It's gotten even worse since you left Homeland Security, and it wasn't good even while you were assigned there, Ms. Chance." Fly turned back to Brad. "Come on, I've got some other things I want you to see."

She led them around the large open room, pointing out different types of communications, encryption, and location gear, most of which were more sophisticated than anything any of them had ever seen before ... equipment that Brad would refer to later as "Buck Rogers stuff."

"That's not all, guys. Follow me over here." Fly led them to a door on the far side that none of them had noticed before. "I call this my drone room," she said, opening the door and leading them into a room that was painted a bright, stark white, walls, floors, and ceiling.

"This one," she said, picking up a solid white drone about a foot across with four propellers on top of it, "is probably the kind of drone you have seen in videos. It's a common type and it is commercially available at a reasonable price." She set the drone down. "These are handy, but they're loud and it's hard to miss them when they are hovering near you. This one has a nice camera and microphone, and it takes beautiful pictures you can see on a laptop in real-time."

She moved down the long table to a square of white linen with several objects spread out on it. "Watch this," she said, reaching for what looked suspiciously like an iPad. She fiddled with the keyboard for a moment, and then all four of them watched in amazement as one of the tiny objects buzzed into life and rose about three feet in the air. She pressed another key on the keyboard and a flat, two-dimensional picture of the four of them appeared on the screen of the controller.

"The picture you are seeing is wide angle and in color. It can be wirelessly broadcast to another device, such as a laptop, a tablet, or even to a smart television screen. The transmitter can send the images through the same satellite communications channels as the earwig uses. In other words, you can be in El Salvador and someone in your Manor House could be seeing what you are seeing in real-time with no noticeable lag."

"Jesus!" Brad was overwhelmed by the possibilities the puny device presented. "That's impressive."

"The guy who made these for me is working on a prototype that looks like a mosquito and is just as small as a real one. The biggest problem he is having so far is creating a battery that is small enough to power it for enough time to make it useful. It already flies, but it only has a range of a couple of hundred meters. That would be useful, but the wind tends to shove it around out in the open air and it's too damned expensive to lose."

"I don't suppose any of these are for sale either, are they?" Vicky asked.

"No, they're not available commercially yet." Fly flashed them a broad grin. "But I'll give them to you if you take that contract and go help those people in El Salvador. I can help you locate those girls."

EIGHT

Day 1, The Manor House, 1500 hours

The three of them were sitting in the study, Willona having gone back to the carriage house to check on Jordan and Nathaniel, the Vings' two young sons. The boys were well behaved, but it didn't do to leave them unsupervised for too long. They were very creative.

"The size of a mosquito?" Ving marveled. "Man, you realize what we could do with something like that?"

"When he gets it into production, the guy's going to make a fortune with the Intelligence agencies!"

Vicky smiled at Brad's remark. The man was a tactical genius, but he would always be a Marine first. He didn't see that the technology Fly Highsmith had just shown them was already past the point where it could be kept secret from anyone outside the military. Big corporations spent billions of dollars on espionage, far more than the government would. Bloated as the government budgets were, corporate pockets were deeper when it came to covert activities. The government liked guns and planes and bombs, tangible things that could be seen created jobs in their districts. Intelligence services went begging, relatively speaking.

"We could sure put the ones she already has to good use, Brad. We sure as hell could have used that little flyer that second time in Fallujah!" Ving was referring to the bloody second battle of Fallujah, where the fighting had been house to house. There had been a severe shortage of K-9s, and Marines had been forced to physically enter buildings and clear them. It had been costly in terms of men, blood, and morale.

"Just think of it, an asset that would allow us to do a real-time recon without exposing us! We could take those bastards flatfooted... They'd never even know we were there until we hit them!"

"Not just on recon, Brad," Vicky told him. "Think bigger. Those things can be operated remotely! Think of having somebody on a computer here in Texas keeping overwatch while you are in movement to contact. No more unexpected contacts, no more having to engage a superior force because you didn't know they were there!"

"It's something to think about, Vicky, and it's awfully tempting. I could take better care of my team members, hell, the earwigs alone would make an enormous difference ... but I still won't take a contract hit. I'm not gonna become like the guys we go after."

"Of course not, Brad, none of us wants that. The other gear she showed us was impressive though. That was smart, asking her to set up our new command and control center in the barn."

"Yeah, the price she quoted me was steep, but thanks to Duckworth we can afford it, Ving. Even with your buy-in we would have been hard-pressed to set this thing up."

Willona had convinced her husband to become a full partner in Team Dallas and had then surprised him with the amount of cash she had squirreled away over the years. Together they had offered Brad more than a million dollars for the partnership, and the cash had made their mission to Borneo substantially easier. Even so, Brad was still recovering from stab wounds suffered during an encounter that could have been avoided if they'd had the assets Fly had showed them. The large, commercially available drone could have helped them avoid the unexpected ambush.

"Here's a problem you don't seem to have taken into consideration, Brad. When you have this all set up, who are you going to leave behind to fly the big drone and keep up the overwatch? If you try to make Jessica do it she's going to raise holy hell." Vicky was smirking at him.

Brad sat straight up in his chair. "I hadn't even thought about that. Who in the hell are we going to get to man the control room?"

"Why just think 'man'? Why don't you give Fly a chance? I'd bet my last dollar she would volunteer her services free if Feng accepts your counter offer."

* * *

The limousine bearing Wu returned within thirty-six hours of the time he had left the Manor House. Once again, the driver remained inside behind the steering wheel while Wu exited and marched to the front door. He knocked, and shortly Brad came to the door wearing jeans and an old U.S.M.C. sweatshirt with the sleeves torn off.

"I didn't expect you back so soon, but I'm glad to see you. Come on in, Mr. Wu, I just put a fresh pot of coffee on and Vicky's making breakfast."

"That really won't be necessary, Mr. Jacobs. I simply came to tell you that Mr. Feng has agreed to your conditions and wishes you to proceed at your earliest convenience."

Brad glanced down at his wrist chronometer. "You may tell Mr. Feng that Team Dallas will be in the air within ten to twelve hours then." He stuck out his hand and shook with Wu.

"I wish you every success, Mr. Jacobs. Good hunting, and good luck!" Wu turned and hurried to the limousine. Brad watched until the sharply dressed Chinese was inside the limo and then turned and bellowed at Vicky. "Round up the team. We are go!" He turned again and watched the limo as it rolled down the long driveway.

Maybe we'll get lucky and that bastard will give us a reason to kill him, he thought.

* * *

"Did you tell him you were unable to contact Mr. Feng?" the driver asked over his shoulder.

"No, I did not," Wu said. "I told them Feng agreed to their terms and they are leaving for El Salvador. Tonight, if Jacobs is a truthful man."

"Do you think that was wise?" The driver was not a 'driver', he was a peer of Wu Li, another lawyer in the firm representing Feng Industries who lost a coin toss and had to play the part of 'driver' in the rented limo.

"It is of no consequence," Wu said with a chuckle. "They 'do not want to kill' El Caiman, they intend to capture El Caiman and bring him to the authorities in Dallas."

"Foolish," the driver said.

"They are as good as dead. El Caiman will chew them up and spit them out for the fishes in Lake LLopango."

"And you can access the funds that cover the retainer check?"

"And I will withdraw the funds for the retainer when they fail to return."

* * *

"There won't be time for me to purchase the new equipment for your C&C center, Brad; I'll have to monitor the operation from my own shop."

"We didn't figure you'd be able to set it up here yet anyway, we've got to sketch out the plans for the contractor to follow before we can set up everything the way you suggested."

"Fine with me. I can pilot the drones from there, and with the earwigs you can talk to me as if I was right there with you. You'll be needing these…" Fly handed Brad a box containing the earwig transceivers and control modules and seven of the iPad looking monitor devices. "And these as well." A larger box contained the full-size drone and a smaller box inside contained a handful of the tiny drones. "Careful with these. They're expensive as hell, but redundancy is critical because they have a tendency to get blown around in the open air. The tiny camera lens is impossible to replace in the field, so the redundancy is doubly critical."

It took over an hour to show them how to use the solar chargers on the tiny drones, but they were surprisingly easy to fly. "Just keep in mind that your flight time is limited. If you don't bring them back before the battery runs down you will very likely lose the thirty grand or so these babies cost, but, more importantly, you'll be giving away the technology that makes them work. An awful lot of people would love to get their hands on one of these."

"We'll treat them as if they were our own."

"You'd better," Fly said with a broad grin. "They are yours now."

NINE

Day 1, The Manor House, 1837 hours

"This is unbelievable," Vicky murmured. She was looking at the blueprints for the house El Caiman had confiscated from the Columbians. It showed the actual security modifications the previous owner had made, including the hardroom where all of the security was run from.

"A lot of what you're looking at I got from a DEA agent. He was in deep cover for over a year when they caught up with him."

"Oh God," Vicky said, her breath caught in her throat. She knew very well what the Columbian cartels did to agents who were exposed. She had known one who had been shipped back to DEA Headquarters in Springfield Virginia ... in little boxes, one piece at a time.

Fly cleared her throat and looked away for a moment. The memory was obviously painful for her. "Steve was a good guy. We ... saw each other for a while before he started taking deep cover assignments. Always looking for the next thrill, never satisfied. He had to keep pushing the envelope. It caught up with him."

"It's like some kind of drug," Brad muttered. "I've known guys like that. They get hooked, and then it takes more and more to satisfy them. It always catches up with them in the end."

The awkward silence that followed was broken by the entrance of a man and a gorgeous blonde Fly recognized from the dossier Walter had given her on Team Dallas. Charlie Dawkins, former State Department agent, and Jessica Paul, Brad's cousin.

"You must be Ms. Highsmith," Jessica said.

"Yes, and please call me Fly." Fly took Jessica's extended hand and shook it then turned to

Dawkins. "You can call me Fly, too, even if you did work for State."

Charlie gave her a warm smile. "I've heard of you. The guys at State speak of you in hushed tones. You're a legend."

"Fly's going to be working with us on this op. She's just given us some super spook equipment and we'll have to teach you how to use it, but right now we need to get the op order written. Pete will be here in a few minutes. He and Jared are in the barn double-checking the MRAZORS, making sure they're ready to go. We had to make some repairs after that trip to Borneo."

"Where's Ving?" Jessica asked.

"Probably stuffing his face with bacon." Vicky was still amused at Ving's insatiable appetite for bacon. He loved the stuff any time, but he always tanked up when Team Dallas was going someplace where he figured it might be in short supply. Willona had bought him an oversized double door refrigerator that he kept stuffed with bacon and a huge gas griddle for his man cave in the carriage house.

“So we’re headed for San Salvador?”

“Yes we are, Jessica, but I don’t want to repeat this so why don’t you and Charlie grab a cup of coffee and take a seat until Pete and Jared come in?”

“Jess can get some, Brad, I’m about coffee’d out. I think I’ll go out to the barn and see if I can help Pete and Jared.” Charlie gave Jessica a peck on the cheek and left the room.

* * *

“You guys need a hand?”

Pete Sabrowski, a former naval aviator in the Corps, was a huge man who could fly anything he could fit his massive frame into. He was tough as nails and a good man in a firefight as well. Brad had served with the man in Afghanistan when Pete had been temporarily grounded due to a mix-up in the results of a routine flight physical. Pete had been assigned to Brad's unit as a Forward Aircraft Controller for a few weeks, and the two men had instantly bonded.

"Nope, we're just about done in here." Pete wiped his hands on a rag and stepped forward to greet his friend and teammate. "How they hangin', Charlie?"

"Low, like always, Pete! Jared get his hands dirty too?"

"Hey, don't act surprised, Charlie!" Jared Smoot stood up from behind one of the MRAZORs, wiping his hands on a rag just as Pete had. "I'm just as good at checking out these fancy ATVs as he is!" Jared, a tall rangy Texan who spoke with a distinct Texas twang and had a taste for his special blend of hot chocolate nearly as legendary as Ving's craving for bacon, was the most incredibly skilled sniper anyone in the team had ever seen.

Jared had come to know and respect the former State Department agent when the plane he and Pete were flying to a hunting lodge in Alaska had gone down and Brad had taken the then much smaller team up to rescue them.

"Brad's about ready to start the mission briefing in the Manor House so we can start crafting the oporder. After you two get over there, all we're waiting on is Ving."

"What's he doin'? Stuffin' his face?"

Charlie laughed. "He's baconating again, at least that's what Vicky was saying. He's afraid they won't have any down there in El Salvador."

"Oh they got bacon," Jared said. "I was down there a few years back, and I know. It ain't like most a them Central American countries. A man can get a regular cup a joe an' bacon an' eggs for breakfast just about anywhere. They make a pretty good cup a hot chocolate too, almost as good as my mix."

"That's high praise coming from you, Jared!" Charlie and Pete both laughed as the lanky Texan licked his lips at the mention of his favorite beverage. The man never went anywhere without a plastic baggie filled with his personal blend of instant hot chocolate somewhere on his person.

The three of them walked out of the barn and up to the Manor House. Ving was already there.

* * *

"Two girls, sisters, were abducted from their home in a suburb of San Salvador six days ago. The abduction was perpetrated by a group of armed men working for a warlord they call El Caiman. These guys are mostly former members of the French Foreign Legion, and they're not your run-of-the-mill South American bad guys. They are pros, the real deal. This guy, El Caiman, real name Simon Leclerc, also a defrocked legionnaire, is an asshole of the first order. He was convicted by a French court martial and sentenced to life in La

Santé Prison in Paris. He escaped and humiliated the Paris cops when he did it." Brad paused to take a breath and let what he had said sink in.

"He's ruthless, and he likes killing innocents just to make sure people get the idea that he's in charge. The government of El Salvador is turning a blind eye to the crap he's pulling because they are either being paid off or they're scared as hell of him."

"Six days ago?" Charlie asked. He knew the statistics as well as anyone there.

"Yes, six days ago. El Caiman, among his other public services, is trafficking in young girls these days. I know the chances are slim that we can find them, but we are going to try to sniff out his pipeline and the place to start is at the front of the operation—the fortress he has confiscated from a local Columbian drug lord."

"He must have balls of steel to pull that off," Ving remarked. "Those cats are bad news an' they don't play."

"They're scared of him too," Fly said quietly. "They made one attempt to take that estate back, and El Caiman killed every last man they sent ... some of their best, by the way."

"This is Felicity Highsmith, former NSA analyst and all-around super spook. She is an expert on Leclerc and she, by way of our client, has brought us some video and documentation I want you to see." He pushed a button on his laptop and then sent the video to a big screen TV he had hastily attached to the laptop. There was no sound, but it wasn't necessary. The video spoke volumes. When it was over, the team sat in shocked silence. Ving finally spoke up.

"Why ain't somebody gone in after this asshole? We got SEALS, we got Rangers, we got Green Beanies ... and, hell, we ain't the only ones with special operators. Why is he gettin' away with this crap?"

"Long story short, Ving, politics," Fly said. "Relations between China and the U.S. regarding tariffs and international trade are at a delicate point, and other nations are involved in the negotiations. We're talking hundreds of billions of dollars here, and nobody is willing to upset the applecart."

"For God's sake, he's an escapee from a French prison!" Charlie burst out. "Why don't they clean up their own mess?"

""They're involved in the negotiations up to their ears, Charlie. Even Interpol won't get involved." Brad was angry and disgusted, and it showed.

"We have elements within our own Congress thwarting every attempt the alphabet agencies have made at resolving this. They're determined to leave this administration swinging in the wind, so they're blocking access to the president. He has no idea what's going on down there and they aren't going to let him until they decide to leak it to the press."

"That's insane!" Jessica was furious. "They're letting those people die over politics?"

"Politics is a dirty business," Fly said sadly. "That's the reason I got out when I did. I've been amassing evidence against Leclerc ever since he started out down there. ICE"—she nodded at Vicky—"is the only agency that really wanted to get involved, but their interest was quashed by a couple of very powerful Senate subcommittee members very quickly. Two department heads were summarily dismissed over their objections."

"I heard about that," Vicky murmured. "I didn't know why they were fired and none of my contacts could or would tell me anything about it."

"More likely wouldn't," Fly said darkly. "People who cross those two have a tendency to have bad 'accidents', and some of them even turn up dead … by their own hand of course. People who have every reason to live."

"That doesn't matter anymore. We're going in. Our client approached us initially with a proposal for a contract hit. I turned that down flat."

It was Jared who spoke up first. "Why Brad? From what I've seen this Caiman guy deserves worse than a bullet in the head."

"Much worse if you ask me!" Jessica's face was a mask of fury. "I'd like some time alone with that sorry bastard myself."

"We're not assassins for hire and that's the end of that subject. We're going after the girls."

"Maybe he'll be foolish enough to fire on us," Jessica retorted. "Then can we shoot him."

Brad gave her a reproving look and then glanced at the others. "If we have any chance at all of taking him prisoner and bringing him to justice we are going to do just that. Are we clear on that?"

There was silence in the room. It was the first time since they had worked together that Brad felt real dissension in the ranks, but he knew they would follow his orders even if they disagreed with him. If it was humanly possible, they would capture El Caiman, even if they all really wanted to kill him. Deep inside, Brad hoped the bastard would fight. If a man ever needed killing, Simon Leclerc did.

* * *

The planning stage of the oporder went smoothly. Fly's documentation was superb, and the photographs the dead ICE agent had sent were grainy because of the button camera he had taken them with, but they gave the team a great idea of what the terrain leading up to the fortress was like. It was evident that the agent had possessed a rudimentary understanding of military tactics because likely avenues of approach and areas of cover and concealment were identified in the pictures.

"How old are these?" Brad asked as he pulled the images up on the screen of his laptop.

"Steve took those a little over a year ago. I've got more recent satellite pictures somewhere, but they aren't as detailed."

"I don't need much detail, I'd just like to see if the landscaping has changed. In particular, here"—he pointed to a squat line of tamarind trees planted at an oblique angle to the main house—"and here." His finger pointed then at the end of a coffee plantation butting up against the property. "Neither will provide much in the way of cover (protection against projectiles), but if they are still there they will provide a little concealment. Those look to be the best ways to approach the main house, but it would save a lot of time if I knew they were there and if they still had leaves."

"I'll check, Brad, but the drones can tell you that. The big drone has a flight time of an hour and a half and a top speed of about forty-five miles an hour. I can do your recon from high enough that the guards won't hear it, and in places where they aren't moving, I can get down all the way to ground level."

"Yeah, but the damned thing is solid white, won't they see it?"

"Not if we spray paint it. It will take a thin coat without adversely affecting the flight characteristics. All you have to do is decide what color would work best for you."

"That's great, but I'd still like some idea of what to expect, it will help with the general concept of the op. We don't think the girls will still be there, so we need to get as close in as we can without being detected. The MRAZORs are really quiet, but this guy has a small army and I don't want to alert them to our presence until I have to."

"That worries me, Brad ... the number of men he has at the fortress. Steve said the bulk of Leclerc's men stay in bunkhouses out in the coffee plantation, several miles from the house, but he keeps a security staff on the grounds at all times. We're talking thirty or more men, counting the monitors inside the hardroom and the inside guards."

Brad grinned at the tiny electronics wizard. "Don't concern yourself with that at all. We go in loaded for bear. You saw my arms room, and you know there are some serious equalizers in the racks."

"I saw. I saw some very sophisticated sniper rifles in there too. Is Jared as good as the reports say he is?"

"I don't think anybody who compiles those reports has the remotest idea of how good Jared actually is. According to the books, the maximum effective range of that Barrett .50 caliber is a little over a mile. The longest confirmed kill on record is about thirty-five hundred meters, or just over two miles. That shot was made by a Canadian Special Forces sniper in Iraq a couple of years ago. I've seen Jared make a shot at about a hundred meters less than that record with his personal Barrett. It took the bullet over ten seconds to reach the target ... and it was a head shot."

"Impressive."

"More than impressive, damn near impossible, but Jared made it."

Fly shook her head. "I don't get it, Brad. You have a guy like that on your team and you could take out Leclerc from so far out they could never catch you. You could make the kill, take the money, and get the hell out of there a couple of million richer without ever having risked the blood of your team members. Why? Why are you putting yourself and your team at risk?"

Brad looked at her for a moment, choosing his words carefully. "I'll admit the money is nice, much more than I ever expected it to be. The thing is we don't do this for the money. We're doing this because we think there is an off-chance that we might be able to track down those girls, and we're doing it because I think we've got a shot at capturing that bastard and bringing him to justice. Those people down there have suffered far too much at his hands, and their government can't or won't help them. Nobody in the world but you and my team seems to give one flying damn about them, and I just don't think that's right."

"But you could be killed…"

Brad shrugged. "Maybe, maybe not. I'm pretty good at what I do, and so are my team members.

It's a job that needs to be done and I think we can do it."

* * *

"Pete, what are you thinking regarding transport?"

"Most of the guys I know down in Central America are flying old Gooney birds or choppers, Brad, but I can make some quick calls and maybe locate something bigger."

Fly grinned. She had some ideas of her own.

* * *

Jessica was steaming. She hated traffickers with a passion, but she hated anyone who would hurt a child just as much. This El Caiman creep had murdered children without a shred of feeling just to show the natives he was in charge, and that made her see red. She had lost her professional cool in Peru and she had treated Guzman with a brutality that had later horrified her.

She knew Brad had not been pleased with the way she had handled Guzman, and she really felt as if she had let him down. She was determined not to let her emotions carry her away in El Salvador, but she was hoping against hope that the bastard would fight them and give them a chance to do what truly needed to be done. Simon Leclerc was a textbook example of a true sociopath, and he had already proved that a high security prison could not hold him, he needed to die.

TEN

Day 2, The Manor House, 0725 hours.

"Pete, you got a line on transport yet?"

"Not yet, Brad. I called A & E down in Cali, but Chief Eggers says he doesn't know of a single C-130 available at the moment. The best he can find is an old Gooney Bird." The Gooney Bird, a Douglass DC-3, was a WWII era aircraft popular with South American drug runners, and it would require some creative adjustments to get the MRAZORs inside. The team had used an old Martin seaplane in Borneo, and onloading and offloading had been time consuming and difficult. Ving had spilled one of the MRAZORs offloading it at the deserted beach where the pilot had landed the seaplane.

"We need something faster than the Gooney Bird, Pete. A C-130 is really what we need because of its ability to land on short, unimproved fields and the ease of offloading the MRAZORs. I'd rather use a C-

141 for the speed, that's a hell of a distance to cover in a hurry, but it doesn't have the short-field capability."

"It's a tall order, Brad, but I'm working on it."

"Still working on transport?" Fly asked from the doorway to the study.

"Yeah, not much luck so far," Brad muttered.

"Maybe I can help with that. I know a guy…"

The "guy" turned out to be a covert operator for the C.I.A. running what amounted to a secret airline between the U.S. and Central and South America. The airline ferried special operators, equipment, munitions and other supplies to the Southern Cone without the bother of clearing customs or even getting permission to operate from sovereign countries. Fly knew his number by heart. Brad could only hear one side of the conversation.

"Herb? Fly here. Listen, is that field near *Suchitoto* still operational? It is? Hey, I need a favor..." There was some trivial banter exchanged before Fly told the man what she needed. "I need one of your 130s, STOVL capable, to transport a seven-man team and two ATVs from Dallas/Fort Worth to Suchitoto. No, I'm not kidding, Herb. Yes, it has to do with that bastard, and, no, I'm not going to tell you who or how... No, it's not sanctioned, but when did you ever worry about that?" She listened for a long moment. "I need this, Herb." Her tone was so hard that even Brad winced. Fly turned to Brad. "How soon?"

"As soon as he can get there, Fly, we're way behind the eight-ball timewise already."

Fly turned back to her cell phone. "ASAP Herb, it's urgent."

* * *

"Wheels up at 1900 hours, guys, we got work to do." Pete looked up from the landline in surprise and then hung up abruptly.

"How'd you manage that?"

"I didn't, Fly did. She got us a C-130, STOVL (short take-off-vertical landing) capable. It'll be at Dallas /Fort Worth at nightfall because they don't want any curious eyes on the bird. Crew will take on a load of fuel at Dyess AFB and then proceed to the transient terminal at DFW. They can only stay on the ground for a short time, so we have to be loaded and ready as soon as it touches down."

"Wow! That woman is handy to have around..."

"Let's get moving!" Brad led the way out to the barn where Jared was putting the finishing touches on the hastily assembled sand table. He had faithfully recreated El Caiman's fortress and grounds from the images Fly had provided using blocks of wood and plastic trees from a kids' toy set that Vicky had purchased some months before for the specific purpose scenes. The mock buildings were not to scale, but they were placed correctly and slides of the actual image were plugged into the big screen TV so they could be flashed on during the oporder briefing.

"Ving not back yet?" Ving had gone with Charlie and Pete to the arms room with one of the MRAZORs to collect the weapons and munitions Brad had specified as well as the team's personal weapons. Jared in particular was picky when it came to his Barrett.

"He should be here any minute, Brad," Jessica said. She lifted her hand to her left ear and touched the near-invisible earwig. "These things are amazing! I can't even feel it in my ear, but I can hear the guys as if they were standing right next to me!"

Brad reached into his pocket and brought out the small box that contained his own earwig and control module. He fastened the module to his belt and then pressed the earwig itself between his hands to warm it up and make it malleable. In a few moments he gently compressed the earpiece and inserted the narrow cylinder into his ear canal and felt it slowly expand until it fit snugly. Surprisingly, it was more comfortable than the foam earplugs he wore on the firing range, and it did not inhibit his normal hearing at all.

"Damn, you coulda helped me with this heavy sonofabitch!" Jared muttered in his ear.

"You too skinny, boy, you needed a lil workout anyway!" Ving chuckled. "You need to eat more bacon ... put some real muscle on that scrawny body a yours!"

Brad placed the thin transmitter disk on the hollow of his throat just as Fly had shown them. "You two through goofin' off yet? Wheels up at 1900!"

"Damn!" Ving said. "I didn't know you had your earwig in yet, Brad! Ain't these things incredible?"

"Play with your new toys later, guys, Jared almost has the sand table ready and Willona is bringing sandwiches out to the barn." Vicky sounded amused.

"Bacon sammiches?"

"For you, Ving, yes. The rest of us are getting BLTs."

"Hot damn!"

* * *

Charlie and Jessica had set up steel folding chairs in front of the sand table and the whole team was sitting and munching as Brad went over the operation by the numbers.

"That's it. Standard P.O.W. snatch if we are extremely lucky, unlikely as that is. Snipe hunt if the girls are already gone. We hit the control room hard in either case. I want hard intel on that pipeline, and, according to Fly's source, that's where Leclerc keeps everything 'business' related."

"What about the offloading plan?"

"We're going to have to wing it, Charlie. All we have is maps of the airfield at Suchitoto. According to the map, the countryside is dotted with unimproved roads and trails, the people have been using them to get to their jobs on the coffee plantations for hundreds of years. All we have to do is follow the ones that run uphill. We can use the GPS to guide us once we get clear of Suchitoto, I don't want to hang around long after we land, Fly tells me those STOVL rocket packs make a hell of a racket."

"They do," Pete said. "I wasn't wearing my headset the first time I flew in one of those and I had a headache for days afterwards."

Brad turned to Vicky. "Remind me to grab a handful of earplugs before we go, please. We'll have to take these earwigs out just before landing and put them back in once we get to a place we can stop for a second."

"Don't wait too long after, Brad; El Caiman's place is only a few miles from Suchitoto and we don't know how far his patrols range out from the fortress. I recommend you get those earwigs back in and launch the big drone as soon as you feel safe enough."

"Do we have enough battery packs to do that? I really want to make sure we can use it at the fortress itself."

"There are three fully charged spares in the case. I showed Vicky and Pete how to swap them out."

"Great!" Brad glanced down at his wrist chronometer. 1400. "Weapons test fire and rehearsals in thirty mikes! Time to saddle up, folks!"

*   *   *

Dallas/Fort Worth International Airport. 1855 hours

The MRAZORs were parked in the shadows in the lee of the transient terminal, and every member of Team Dallas including Brad was fidgeting nervously. The scream of jet engines was pounding in their ears, and Jessica was wondering whether she should use the earplugs Brad had passed out. She glanced over at Vicky, who was in the other MRAZOR sitting in the front seat with Brad. Vicky smiled back at her and Jessica could see the orange foam plugs lodged in her ears. Without further hesitation Jessica shoved the foam plugs into her ears and was immediately relieved.

"I hear it!" Ving growled. He cranked his MRAZOR and slipped it into gear. The big four-engine turboprop had the bare minimum aviation lights flashing on as the pilots feathered the props and lowered the plane onto the runway. The aircraft slowed quickly and taxied onto the pan in front of the transient terminal. They could see the interior lights and the crew chief standing on the tailgate, and Brad cranked his MRAZOR and raced toward the craft before it had even stopped moving.

As soon as he came to a full stop at the front of the cargo compartment the crew chief and loadmaster began to strap the MRAZOR down to the eyelet rings on the aluminum floor. The crew chief shouted into his headset as Ving brought the second ATV to a halt and the C-130 began to roll back out to the runway before the tailgate was even raised. By the time the pilots had lined up for takeoff, the crew chief had raised the tailgate and taken his seat in the orange webbed seats along the fuselage. In no time at all they were in the air in a steep climb that is the hallmark of the C-130.

* * *

The chief and the crewman wore nondescript overalls with no markings of any kind, which Brad assumed was par for the course for C.I.A. types running a clandestine airline. Brad felt the aircraft begin to lose altitude four hours into the flight and glanced over at the crew chief, who had not said a word during the entire flight. The chief held up three fingers and then motioned for Brad and the others to remain seated.

Vicky leaned over and spoke above the muted roar of the engines. “I thought we were going to get out of this beast as quickly as possible.”

“We are, but this isn’t going to be like any landing you’ve ever made before. When you feel the wheels touch down, tuck in your chin and hold on to the webbing of the seat. Got it?” Vicky nodded.

Brad and Ving slipped on specially modified prototype models of the EOTech GPNVG (Ground

Panoramic Night Vision Goggle) that Fly had wheedled out of another of her industrial contacts. The devices looked weird with their four optical tubes poking out in front, but the ninety-seven-degree field of view and the spectacular light gathering qualities of the optics made the expensive little devils invaluable.

A moment later, the wheels touched down with a resounding thump, and then the nose wheels touched. Immediately there was a roaring sound and the entire team felt as if they were being slammed forward by a giant hand. The plane screamed to a halt, the tailgate lowering as they clambered aboard the MRAZORs. The crewman snapped open the quick release tie downs at a dead run and Team Dallas was roaring down the tailgate wide open. None of them saw the spectacular light show when the C-130's booster rockets kicked in and blasted the massive plane into the air. It had not stayed on the ground long enough to stop rolling completely.

Brad headed for a rutted 'unimproved' road at the southwest corner of the old airstrip as fast as he dared in the dark, Ving right behind him. Everyone but Brad and Ving was replacing their earwigs, but it was difficult in the wildly jouncing MRAZORs. When they were more than a mile from the airstrip, Brad stopped for a second to put his own earwig in.

"...you need to tell him to stop and put his earwig in and launch the drone, Vicky," Fly was saying.

"He just pulled off to the side of this goat trail. I'll tell him."

"I heard you, but I'm not comfortable stopping long enough to launch the drone." He slammed the MRAZOR into gear and stomped on the throttle, racing back onto the road. "I'll stop in another mile or so. I'd forgotten just how loud those planes were. If there's anyone around here, they heard that bird when it landed and took off."

"Brad, it's not just El Caiman's guys you need to watch out for down there! The PNC runs patrols looking for the *transportistas,* you have the *transportistas* themselves, and you have the gangs to worry about. Nighttime in EL Salvador is no place to be running around in the dark without eyes."

"We'll just have to chance it, Fly. I'm getting bad vibes right now and my gut is telling me to get the hell out of here in a hurry."

Jared's Barrett remained in its carrying case, strapped securely to the cargo compartment of the MRAZR, but he had taken out a CAR-4 and looped the sling over his arm. He, like the others, had four magazine pouches stuffed with thirty-round magazines on his web belt and one in the magazine well of the CAR-4. Everyone but Ving and Brad had already locked and loaded. Vicky and Jessica were quickly remedying that, placing weapons in the scabbards located on the driver's side dash of each of the MRAZORs.

"As soon as you're finished with that, get out your monitor and check the GPS. I'm bearing to the southwest and uphill as best I can tell, but I need to get oriented toward the fortress as soon as possible."

"I'll try, Brad, but it's going to be hard to read. This damned go kart is bouncing around too much to hold it steady. These roads aren't as big as they looked in the photos."

"Unimproved roads my ass, these are goat trails!" Brad mumbled under his breath. There were tracks on the rough dirt surface of the road, but they were by and large caused by human feet instead of by vehicles.

* * *

Even with the night vision goggles Brad had to go slower than he wanted to. There were dozens of foot trails branching off the road to the southwest, but he was unsure of whether they would remain passable for the incredibly sure-footed MRAZORs. He wished he'd had more time to study the terrain, but time was running desperately short for the two girls and time was a luxury commodity that he just didn't have. That was the biggest reason they were almost wiped out.

The larger road was graded and flat, and it intersected the unimproved road they were traveling along. The problem was that, according to the maps and the aerial photographs, it wasn't supposed to be there at all. Brad locked up the brakes and signaled for three-hundred-sixty-degree security.

Jared was out of the rear MRAZOR like a shot, taking the left side and racing several meters into the wood line before dropping to one knee. Ving was right behind him. Pete and Charlie went to the right, spreading out into the woods, Charlie facing the rear. Jessica glanced wildly at Brad and Vicky then hurried over to take rear watch behind Ving.

"The GPS says we are right where we're supposed to be."

"I wonder how old those aerial photographs were. There was no indication of a road here at all. Are you sure that thing is working right?"

"The GPS is still working right," Fly's voice came through the earwigs as clearly as if she was standing beside them. "Something's wrong, Brad. Those aerial photos are less than a month old. Just how big is this road?"

"It's as wide as my driveway, but it's got a prepared bed and it's graded like they intend to pave the damned thing."

"Get the drone out, Brad, I need to see this. Building a road out of nothing takes a buttload of money, and we need to know who did this."

“Hey, Fly, I’m not on an intelligence gathering mission for the government, I’m here to chase down two helpless kids!”

“Let me rephrase, Brad,” Fly said drily. “You need to know who did this. From your position on my GPS monitor and your direction of travel, that road has to be pointed directly at El Caiman’s villa. If so, you may have just stumbled onto the next part of his pipeline.”

“And if it’s part of his pipeline,” Vicky finished, “he may have brought in more mercs.”

“What it probably means is that he’s increasing the volume of his trafficking...”

“Or he’s running drugs or guns now...” Vicky added.

“Or both...” Fly finished.

It didn’t matter. The new black carryall came out of the darkness running parking lights only at reckless speed, the sound of its engine muffled by the dense vegetation on either side of the road. It came so suddenly that there was no time to seek concealment.

Brad froze in position beside the MRAZORs, knowing that night vision depended largely on movement, and for a moment he thought his luck would hold, but it didn't. There was a shout from the carryall and the side doors flew open as it skidded to a halt. Men poured out the side of the vehicle, guns blazing as Brad and Vicky dove for the ditch.

Jared was the first to return fire, spraying three- to six-round bursts into the gunmen. They were fairly well trained. They sought cover and went to ground and spread out firing back at Jared, not wild automatic fire but aimed fire. Unfortunately for them, they were not well trained enough to expect the perimeter defense Team Dallas had established at the halt.

Ving and Jessica returned fire right after Jared did, but the gunmen were caught in the enfilade fire provided by Charlie and Pete. It took longer than they would have expected, because the gunmen had fought from behind cover, but eventually the only sound left was the sound of the running engine of the carryall.

Jared stood up and signaled that he was going to check the vehicle, and Pete circled around to the far side at the same time, both men approaching the carryall with weapons at the ready. Jared peeked inside and then snatched the door open. The driver sprawled out onto the ground, the top of his head missing.

“Clear,” Jared said quietly. The transmitter on his throat picked up the sound of his voice and transmitted it. The others rose from their places of cover and Brad called out.

“Everybody okay?”

One after another, they called out their names until Brad turned to Vicky, who was wiping mud from her hands and the front of her nightsuit.

"Shit! Now what are we gonna do? They had to have heard this at the fortress. This place is gonna be swarming with mercs in no time at all."

"We don't know that, Brad…"

"Yeah, you don't know that, Brad!" Fly's voice sounded worried. "Is everybody all right?"

"Yeah Fly, we're okay, but I think the mission may be blown."

"Don't be so sure, leatherneck, and don't give up so easy. You've got assets you haven't used yet. Get the hell off that goat trail and send up the drone!"

"I should have thought of that!" Brad was disappointed in himself. His ability to think through difficult tactical problems and find workable alternatives was a point of personal pride. Improvise, adapt, overcome! His train of thought was interrupted by a cry from Jessica.

"Brad! Quick, get over here!"

Brad raced toward the rear of the carryall, Vicky close behind him.

"There's a girl in here, Brad! She's hurt!"

Brad climbed into the carryall and saw a young girl who had been beaten so badly her own mother would never have recognized her. Her face was blood streaked, puffy, and swollen, and she was unconscious ... but she was breathing. Jessica was frantically trying to wipe the blood off her face with a sterile wet wipe from the first aid pouch at her waist.

"She's missing a couple of teeth and her lip is badly cut, but she's breathing." The girl's breath was raspy, and even unconscious, she was flinching with each breath. "She may have a broken rib or two, but I think she's going to be okay."

"We won't know that for sure until she regains consciousness," Jared said. "She's been worked over pretty good, but I really can't tell if she's got a concussion until I can get a look at her eyes." He shook his head in disgust. "She needs a doctor."

"We're not going to find one out here," Vicky muttered.

Ving ran up behind the carryall. "I checked the road a ways. No sound of vehicles or people at all. Dead silence from the direction of Leclerc's place. Didn't see any lights either, and you'd think there'd be some kind of glow in the sky from it out here in the country like this."

"The drone!" Fly screeched into their ears. "Stop guessing, dammit! Use your freakin' assets!"

"She's right! Get the MRAZORs into the wood line. Enter from different spots and then parallel the wood line for about thirty meters while Vicky and I launch the damn drone! Ving, you and Jess take care of the girl." With that, he ran to his MRAZOR and grabbed the case with the large drone. With Vicky's help, he dragged it into a clearing about twenty meters inside the wood line and they began to unpack it.

Jared and Pete moved the MRAZORs into the woods per Brad's instructions and then went back to the carryall. They searched the bodies to see if they could find any useful information on them.

"These guys ain't wearin' them black uniforms with the gold gator on 'em, Jared."

Jared frowned in the moonlight as he rolled one of the bodies over. "They may not be El Caiman's men, but they were trained, and they were carrying some pretty high-dollar hardware." He lifted an HK MP7A1 with a suppressor, extended magazine and Elcan reflex sight.

"Damn man! Were they all carrying those?"

"Yeah, and this carryall can't have more than a couple of hundred miles on it. If it wasn't for the blood, the vomit, and the smell of powder, this thing would still have that new car smell." The girl had obviously thrown up in the back as she was being beaten.

"Transportistas, Jared, those are transportistas!" Fly said. "They work on contract for the cartels or whoever pays them best. I don't know anything about El Caiman's pipeline, but I'd bet my last dime they are part of it. Check 'em good, they may have something good on a scrap of paper. As a matter of fact, see if you can gather up everything left in that carryall that has any kind of writing on it ... oh, and get pictures."

"Woman don't want much," Ving grumbled even as he started about doing what she asked.

"I heard that, Ving!"

“Oh Lord, she’s worse than Willona!” Ving touched the transmitter disk in the hollow of his throat. “I don’ think I’m gonna like these gizmos as much as I thought I would, brother.”

Jared smiled and touched his mike as well. “I’m with you, Ving, but I kinda like ’em sassy. She’s kinda cute too.”

“Oh Lord!” Ving intoned, rolling his eyes.

* * *

The drone launched quickly and easily, and Brad and Vicky watched it soar silently between the treetops and then above them.

“You got it, Fly?” Brad asked.

“You don’t have to yell, Brad, I can hear you even when you whisper. Yeah, I got it. Just watch your monitor.”

Vicky touched her throat mike with her forefinger. "Guess I'll have to be a little more careful when we stand down wearing these things."

"We'll take 'em off when we stand down," Brad snarled.

"I heard that too!"

Brad snorted in disgust, but his eyes were drawn to the monitor Vicky was holding in her hand. The screen showed a large villa sitting close to the top of a mountain. There were sentries inside a gatehouse some three hundred meters downhill from the villa.

"Can you get a little closer or zoom in on that gatehouse?"

"I can do both."

A few seconds later, the picture zoomed in from a lower altitude and the field of resolution showed the inside of the small gatehouse with miraculous detail. There were two men sitting inside. A bored looking heavyset blond man was sitting at a desk reading a book, and a younger, slimmer man was leaning back in an armchair with earbuds plugged into a cell phone and he appeared to be talking.

"Doesn't look like they heard anything, does it?"

A radio set and what appeared to be some kind of control panel covered with lights, all a steady, unblinking green, sat on the top of the steel desk. There was little else in the room.

"No, it doesn't. Fly, check the perimeter."

The image on the monitor grew smaller and the drone began to move toward the eastern perimeter, which was marked by a path consisting of two ruts, obviously a trail made by a mounted patrol just outside a wooded area. They were interrupted by a commotion over by the MRAZORs.

"What's that?" Brad asked, but Jessica was already running toward the sound.

"Go ahead, Brad, check it out. I got this," Fly said. "I can play back anything I spot for you, and I can tell you if there's something urgent you need to see."

"And you can take the damned monitor with you," she muttered to herself. *I can see this is going to take some getting used to for him. He's not used to this technology, he doesn't fully comprehend what it can do for him yet.*

The injured girl was conscious and babbling crazily, and it was plain to see that she was terrified. Jessica was trying to calm her down, but the men had backed away from her.

"I couldn't make any sense out of what she was sayin', Brad. Her mouth is a train wreck and she's hysterical."

"After what she's been through, Jared, I'm not surprised that she's scared of men. Did you move those bodies into the woods?"

"Yeah we did, or at least Ving and Pete went back to do it."

"We movin' 'em now man. Pete's gonna try to drive this carryall in as deep as he can. When he's done, we're gonna camouflage the back so's nobody can see it from the road ... leastways, not at night." It was a little eerie to be able to hear everyone as if they were standing next to him, but Brad was seeing it as a definite advantage. A firefight at night was one of the most difficult things in the world to control, but the one they had just finished had gone off without a hitch, even though it had come out of the blue.

Jessica had calmed the girl down some, but she still wasn't coherent. Brad looked at her disfigured face a little more closely and was startled to see that she was Oriental. *No, it couldn't be... That would be too much like luck, and I don't really believe in that. Those girls are long gone, but maybe this one can tell us more about the pipeline.*

"Brad?"

"Yeah Vicky?"

"There's drugs in the carryall, a lot of them."

"Crap! I'm betting the carryall is tagged! They were too well equipped! Everybody saddle up, we need to get out of here in a hurry!"

"Good move, Brad," Fly's voice spoke in their ears.

"Somebody's coming out of the villa, two more carryalls and a car—and they look like they're in a hell of a hurry."

ELEVEN

Day 2, El Caiman's Villa. 2351 Hours

Piccard knocked on the library door and then entered. El Caiman was wearing a smoking jacket and held a large snifter of brandy in one hand as he smoked a fat black Cuban cigar.

"We've lost contact with the carryall. Radio operator says he heard gunfire and some yelling but nothing clear."

"Where are they?"

"We don't know. They took the new carryall and the transponder hasn't been installed yet."

Leclerc was furious, but he didn't let it show on his face. The girl was unimportant, but there was a massive consignment of cocaine for the Columbians concealed beneath the floorboards of the carryall. The local PNC was permitted, by agreement, to take the occasional shipment, usually a very small one, but the agreement specifically excluded the 'seizures' anywhere near the villa. This was a violation of the agreement, and one which could not be tolerated. It had to be the PNC, no one else had the balls to take on one of his crews, even the ones in unmarked carryalls and out of uniform.

They hadn't been gone long enough to get far. Diego, the Spaniard who was making his first run as supervisor, had taken the new vehicle instead of one of the others, something he should have known better than to do. That would have some serious consequences for the man. In the meantime, he needed to find that carryall and quickly. Resistance of any kind to his will was intolerable and had to be met with massive retribution immediately, but it had to be against the perpetrators, pour encourager les autres.

"Find the carryall, Lucien, find it quickly!" He rose and headed for his bedroom. There was bloody work to be done this night, but first Lucien had to find out if the carryall had been taken by the PNC or if Diego had gotten greedy. Someone was going to pay regardless, and El Caiman would exact the price personally.

* * *

Piccard led the two carryalls full of men down the driveway past the gatehouse and turned left toward the new road El Caiman had recently completed, cutting the travel time to the highway to Suchitoto or Ichanquezo in half. Both were checkpoints on El Caiman's 'pipeline', which he used to export or import, well, anything from guns to drugs to girls. He wasn't fully focused at the moment, though he should have been. Leclerc had been dressed in his 'playboy' outfit, and Piccard suspected he had been about to despoil Chu Hua. The thought of Leclerc rutting on that beautiful young girl incensed him. Since he had first seen her the desire to have her for himself had been growing until it had become an obsession.

"There, take the turnoff onto the new road," he instructed his driver. The driver, a new kid recently taken into the organization, was not as skillful at driving as he'd claimed to be, and he locked up the brakes before skidding into the turn onto the new road. He tried to make up for his error by overcorrecting and then veered wildly before he got it back under control. Piccard said nothing. They traveled almost two miles before Piccard saw the tail end of the new black carryall sticking out of the wood line beside the road. "Stop!"

The former legionnaires in the carryalls behind them needed no instruction; they piled out of the vehicles and fanned out to either side of the road, approaching the carryall cautiously, weapons at the ready.

It wasn't long before the bodies were discovered.

"Diego won't get another chance to supervise," one of the mercs remarked.

"Neither will any of the others. Looks like they're all dead."

"Check the... Never mind, I'll do it myself." Lucien walked over and opened the secret compartment beneath the floor of the carryall and was surprised to see the duct tape-wrapped packages of cocaine still there. The bricks of cocaine were inserted into bags of freshly ground coffee beans and then the bags were covered with duct tape in an attempt to disguise the smell. Most of the time it worked, but occasionally one of the better trained dogs would sniff it out anyway. He was about to have the men come secure the drugs when the first glimmer of a plan popped into his mind. Leclerc suspected the PNC was behind this, but apparently whoever had ambushed the carryall was only interested in the girl. If he could make Leclerc believe the coke had been the target of the ambush, he would punish the local PNC commandant and Piccard could remove the cocaine later for himself. The cartel would give him enough money for the coke to go somewhere Leclerc couldn't find him, an island maybe ... and he would find a way to take Chu Hua with him. It was a brilliant idea, if he could pull it off. The risk was enormous, but Chu Hua would be worth it.

"Push the carryall into the woods and camouflage it," he ordered. The mercs weren't the kind of men to question their orders. El Caiman paid well, but it didn't pay at all to disregard his orders. Piccard spoke with El Caiman's voice. The carryall was camouflaged in short order.

* * *

"No sign of the carryall, but we found the men. All dead," Piccard said tersely into his cell phone. There was a moment of silence and Piccard could imagine the look on Leclerc's face. He had been with the man long enough to have seen the maniacal fury on his face when he was crossed. Piccard was one of the few who had survived one of El Caiman's rages.

"I'll be waiting for you here, but make it fast, Lucien. We have work in Soyapango."

* * *

Lucien did not let the kid drive back to the villa. Leclerc was waiting for them in front of the villa when the Jeep rolled up in the circular drive, and he entered the vehicle without saying a single word. They had reached the gatehouse before Leclerc spoke.

"You know where Commandant Diaz lives?"

Lucien nodded.

"Go there, and go quickly." The tight-lipped Leclerc stared straight ahead, looking neither left nor right as Piccard expertly piloted the Jeep down Carretara Suchitoto, the road toward San

Bartolome Perulapia, and then right on Carretara Panamericana to Soyapango. The two carryalls of mercs followed close behind them.

Piccard's mind was on other things as he drove. How to recover the cocaine wasn't a real issue. Leclerc thought the PNC had it, and he had no reason to believe that the carryall had not been destroyed in the attack. Eventually one of the mercs would mention it or Leclerc would ask one of them, but Piccard intended to be long gone before the subject came up. The hard part was going to be finding a way to get Chu Hua out of the villa without anyone noticing it. The guys in the hardroom monitored the comings and goings of everyone who came into the villa except for El Caiman himself. His private rooms had no cameras, no bugs. He was a private man.

* * *

Colonel Roberto Diaz lived in a Mediterranean-style villa in an exclusive neighborhood on the shores of Lake LLopango, near Club Didea. The Jeep stopped in the dooryard of the expensive home and Leclerc did not wait for Piccard to open the door. He bounded out like a bridegroom racing for his wedding bed, and when he reached the massive double doors he didn't bother to knock. He opened them with his boot.

"Diaz!" he roared. Piccard watched Leclerc unholster the engraved, nickel-plated, pearl-handled Colt .45 Government model handgun and stride into the foyer of the mansion as if he owned the place. In a way, that was appropriate. It was El Caiman's bribe money that had built the place.

The mercs deployed around the house and Piccard followed El Caiman with three of his best mercenaries into the house.

"Diaz!" Leclerc roared again.

Diaz came out of a sitting room dressed much as El Caiman had been when Piccard had given him the news of the missing shipment. "What is the meaning of this, El Caiman?" He was angry, but he was more afraid than angry.

Leclerc pointed the big pistol at Diaz' forehead. "Roberto, you disappoint me." He pulled the hammer back. The sound of it was deafening in the room. Diaz dropped to his knees, seeing only death in the warlord's eyes.

"What is wrong? Tell me what I have done!"

"Get up off your knees, Roberto, you know what you have done, and you know what happens to people who cross me."

Diaz got to his feet, pleading for mercy for an act he had no knowledge of, but El Caiman was unmoved.

"Outside Roberto!"

Diaz walked woodenly toward the smashed and broken doors, he was crying and still pleading for

Leclerc to tell him what was wrong. Leclerc simply smiled the thin-lipped smile he wore when he was about to kill and said nothing.

Piccard drove the Jeep, Diaz in the front passenger seat, Leclerc in the rear seat with his pistol pressed against the wailing man's head. They went to an open field outside Soyopango, where Piccard parked and doused the lights.

"Turn them back on, Lucien, I want to see his face."

Leclerc frog-marched the colonel to a spot in front of the headlights and Lucien flicked them to high beam. Sweat and tears mingled on Diaz' face as Leclerc forced him to his knees once more.

"Lucien, your knife..." Leclerc held out his hand and Piccard removed his treasured Arkansas Toothpick, handmade by a legendary American knife maker, Walter Doane "Bo" Randall Jr., a year before his death. The knife had been a present from his uncle, given to him on the occasion of his elevation to the rank of "legionnaire". He knew what Leclerc was about to do, he had seen it before and it sickened him.

The interrogation began, and it lasted a long, long time. Colonel Roberto Diaz did not get to go home.

* * *

"Did you believe what he said, Lucien?"

Piccard, driving slowly back along the Carretara Panamericana, took a long time to answer. By the time Leclerc had finished with his ghoulish torture routine, Diaz had been saying whatever he thought the warlord wanted to hear. Piccard knew the colonel had been telling the truth from the beginning, the PNC had not been involved. Whoever had ambushed the carryall had shown no interest in the cocaine, they had been after the girl ... a thought that had just occurred to him during the 'interrogation'. That put a new wrinkle in his plans for Chu Hua; he would have to do whatever he was going to do as soon as possible.

"I think he was telling the truth to start with." El Caiman laughed, a short, nasty laugh. "I am rarely wrong, Lucien, and I hate being wrong. You know what makes me angrier than being wrong? I hate being wrong in front of my men, Lucien, it is humiliating."

Piccard kept his mouth shut and his eyes on the road. Leclerc was at his most dangerous when he spoke this way, almost hissing the words out. When he got like this, no one was safe from his wrath. He was totally unpredictable.

"This poses a whole new problem for me, doesn't it, Lucien? Who else would have the balls to intercept one of my shipments? More importantly, how did they know about it?" Leclerc's voice took on a menacing tone. "You know what I think? I think one of my people has gotten greedy, Lucien. And that is a bad thing. A very bad thing." His hand was gripping the butt of the big .45 and Lucien was getting really nervous. Did he know? Did he even suspect? He did the only thing he could think of to do.

"Whoever it was cannot have gotten far. I think we need to calculate how far they might have been able to go and then send out search teams in every direction as fast as they can go and then start to search inward ... cut them off."

Leclerc stared at his number two in astonishment. "If they're running from us, how in the hell do you think we could possibly get ahead of them and search inward? Have you taken leave of your senses, Lucien? You know better!"

Piccard's guts were knotted. If El Caiman started the search close in, the mercs who had been with him when he found the carryall would rat him out. He had to find a way to keep them separate from the ones doing the searching at all costs. The solution came to him in a blinding flash.

"I apologize," he said soothingly. "I wasn't thinking straight. We should dispatch the rest of the crew in the barracks and set them on the chase right now, by cell phone. We need to take the crew we have with us back to the villa and then augment the perimeter security with them. If whoever did this had the balls to take down one of our shipments, they might not be running away at all, they might be getting ready to hit the villa right now!"

El Caiman looked stunned. The idea that his villa, his fortress, might be attacked had not crossed his mind. "Do it!" he commanded. Then he leaned forward and gripped the dashboard with his fingers so tightly that his knuckles whitened.

Piccard hated using his cell phone when driving, especially at the speeds he was pushing the Jeep at, but he did it anyway. The senior supervisor, Stefan Kubiak, at the converted coffee plantation bunkhouse several miles from the villa answered on the first ring and listened carefully to Piccard's instructions. He responded with one word and hung up. Piccard slammed the cell phone into his breast pocket and stomped on the accelerator.

* * *

The Jeep skidded to a stop at the gatehouse, sending the front ends of the carryalls behind him nose-diving towards the road surface. Piccard leaped out and started barking commands to the merc leaders in the carryalls. In moments the leaders had broken down the men into three squads of ten and dispersed them. Then the carryalls rolled up to the concrete apron behind the villa, and the groups began to separate. One squad went to the immense garage where spare ATVs were stored for the roving guards, one squad went inside to reinforce interior security, and the third squad went to the small bunkhouse normally used by the onsite guards for sleeping between shifts.

Piccard harangued the gatehouse guards for a moment before jumping back into the Jeep to take El Caiman up to the villa. Leclerc had not said a word.

When the Jeep lurched to a stop, El Caiman stalked into the house and straight to his hardroom. One glance at the warlord told the hardroom operators to focus on their various computers and monitors. They knew better than to greet him or engage in their usual banter when they saw the storm clouds on his face. The room became absolutely silent except for the humming and buzzing of the machines and the occasional chirp or blare from the radio transmissions of the roving guards. Piccard kept his face a solid mask of indifference, even while his mind was racing, trying to work out a viable plan.

* * *

Leclerc sat down at his polished mahogany desk and forced himself to do the deep breathing exercises that calmed him. He had been looking forward to the torture session with Diaz. Inflicting pain and watching human suffering had given him pleasure since he was a young man. He didn't understand why it gave him pleasure, but it did and he'd never questioned it. Diaz had ruined the session for him, and that, coupled with the loss of a multimillion-dollar shipment of uncut cocaine to parties unknown, had sent him flying into a rage. He needed to think, and at the moment he could not do so clearly.

TWELVE

Day 3, 5 Miles Southwest of Suchitoto, El Salvador, 0114 hours

The Mrazor is a rugged vehicle with a three-cylinder turbocharged diesel engine, designed to stand up against anything an infantryman can come up against, but it isn't bulletproof.

Brad stood in front of the Mrazor, staring down at the steam leaking out of one of the coolant hoses. The tiny red overheating light had come on just after he had noticed the steam rising. He had driven the ATV into a thicket out of habit. Concealment during stops on movement to contact was second nature to him. Ving had done the same with the other Mrazor, twenty or so meters behind him.

"What's up?" Jared, the most mechanically inclined member of Team Dallas, already had his head down inside the engine compartment, checking to see where the steam was coming from. "Oh hell," he snorted. "Looks like it got nicked by a stray bullet during the firefight, Brad."

"Nothing a mechanical genius such as yourself can't deal with." Despite the tenseness of the situation, Brad was grinning.

"Not a problem. It won't last forever, but a little duct tape will get us where we need to go and back. It can't be more than a few miles to the fortress."

"Well, I hope you know where some is," Ving said quietly. "The last time I remember seeing it, the damned roll was lying on top of the packing crate we took that air filter out of before we went in to meet Fly."

"Oh shit!"

"You'd better find a reasonable substitute quick," Fly's voice said in their ears. "Looks like they've doubled or maybe tripled the roving guards, and you guys are a lot closer than you think you are. Geez Brad, don't you guys use the GPS?"

Brad checked the monitor on his device and swore. At best they were only a mile and a half from the villa.

"Since I'm already spreading bad news, you guys ready for some more?"

"Oh Lord, what now, woman?" Ving was having a little trouble getting used to Fly's voice in his ear. He couldn't see her, and he tended to forget she was there. When she spoke up unexpectedly, it was as if she was inside his head, and that was, well, that was pretty damned spooky. It made him jumpy and a little irritable.

"I can't be sure, but I think I might have caught an outgoing transmission during your little skirmish back there. I've been trying to run it down, but I haven't had any luck so far. You should probably proceed on the premise that your presence has been detected and you are compromised."

"Shit!"

"I set the drone down in the top of one of those coffee bushes to conserve battery power. There's plenty left, I can put her back in the air whenever you want."

"Hey, what about this?" Jessica walked toward the first Mrazor, a small packet in her hand. "This was in the fording kit." It looked like an old time bicycle tube repair kit, which is essentially what it was. There was a metal grater to rough up the surface and a vulcanizing rubber patch.

"We can try it," Jared said doubtfully. "I don't know how long it will hold, though, not under constant heat and pressure."

"Wrap it with this," Charlie said, producing a remnant of a roll of electrical tape from the hip pocket of his nightsuit. "It's not much, but it may help it hold long enough to get us somewhere we can find a replacement hose."

"We have to do something, Jared, we can't stay here. If we're still up here come daylight we're dead meat, especially if Fly is right about us being compromised."

"I can try, Brad, but I can't promise we're going to get very far."

"Just do the best you can, Jared." Brad looked up at the sky for a moment, thinking. "Fly, get that drone in the air. See if you can find us a toolshed or a barn, someplace where they might store equipment, machinery, something like that."

"Roger that!"

"I need a couple of alcohol pads from one of the first aid kits to clean this hose off before I can put the patch on it."

"Here," Vicky said, handing him a couple of the foil wrapped packets from the back seat of the Mrazor. She was tending to the girl, who had finally stopped crying and was just beginning to comprehend that she was no longer a prisoner.

"How is she?"

"Doing better than I expected, Brad. She's still in shock, and she's been pretty badly beaten. Trying to talk but she's got several broken teeth and her mouth is swollen so badly I can't make out what she's saying."

* * *

Ving was watching Brad, concerned. He had known Brad longer than anyone on the team except Jessica, and more than once the two of them had worked together wounded and in dire circumstances. He was as close to Brad as a brother, and he knew when the man was hiding his pain.

A terrorist named Ahmad Hamdani had stabbed Brad in the side with a wicked curved steel blade called a karambit when they had rescued Bill Duckworth from a training camp in Borneo. It had been a nasty wound, and Brad was still hurting from it. Ving wasn't sure if the others were aware of it, but he knew the signs. He also knew better than to try to talk to Brad about it. His friend would be embarrassed if he knew Ving was aware of his discomfort.

Even so, Ving intended to keep an eye on him. Brad always said that everything was a weapon, but pain detracted from any warrior's abilities. There was a fight coming, Ving could feel it in his bones. El Caiman was one bad dude, and he wouldn't just let them waltz in and piss in his Cheerios. He had a lot of assets available to him, and from what Ving had seen, they were not amateurs. The Légion étrangère had a well-deserved reputation for turning out some really tough and highly competent troops, and most of El Caiman's mercs were veterans of real combat in some real hellholes. This wasn't going to be a walk in the park.

He glanced at Brad again out of the corner of his eye and sighed quietly. Ving was worried.

* * *

Jared removed the hose from the Mrazor's radiator with the Leatherman Coyote Signal Multitool he carried in a nylon pouch on his web belt. He had actually discovered the gadget when he was at a gunsmith's shop having the trigger mechanism on his Barrett .50 polished and fine-tuned. The multitool, true to its name, had nineteen blades with various functions, and it had been an extremely useful addition to his combat kit.

The alcohol pads Jessica had given him had done a fair job of cleaning the hose off because the hose was, after all, not very old. He heated the patch very carefully with a lighter to soften it up before peeling the protective covering off of it then wrapped the patch around the curved surface as best he could. Lifting a corner of the top covering, he set the edge aflame and heard the characteristic sputter of the vulcanizing process as it burned. Cupping his hands around the low flame to keep the light from escaping, he waited until the sputtering stopped. He folded the Leatherman up and put it back in its carrying case before wrapping the electrical tape around the outside of the patch.

“There,” he muttered, standing up to stretch. “Don’t know how long the sonofabitch is gonna hold, but it was worth a shot.”

“Gonna need some coolant to replace what got out too,” Pete observed.

“We can put some water from the canteens in it till we can get more.”

"I'll worry about that when I get it back on. I sure hope Fly can find us someplace we can scavenge some hose and a little antifreeze."

"Good luck with that, sniper boy! It don't get below seventy degrees here even in the winter."

"I been here before, Ving. They gotta use antifreeze here in the hot weather ta keep the water pumps lubricated, 'specially on heavy farm equipment."

"No luck so far, guys," Fly said in their ears. "I've seen a couple of possibles but they're too dang close to the villa. Lotta lights on for this time of the morning, and in a couple of hours these farmers are going to start getting up to slop their hogs or armadillos or whatever."

"Keep lookin', woman, we in a bit of a tight down here..." *That woman is downright spooky!* Ving shook his head. He didn't know if he'd ever get used to having Fly in his head.

* * *

Fly altered the flight path of the drone, putting it on an azimuth that took her high above the unimproved road instead of on a straight line toward the thicket where Brad and the team were working on the ailing Mrazor. There were isolated shacks dotted along the roadway, but hardly any showed any signs of life yet. These farmers were so poor that they probably couldn't even afford electricity anyway. There was no farm equipment outside any of them anyway as far as she could see, even in the bright moonlight. She decided to take the drone to a higher altitude.

The light gathering characteristics of the optics on the drone were not as good as they could have been, and she made a mental note to discuss that with Al Horowitz, the builder. Like anyone who has ever ridden in a chopper at night, she knew that at an altitude of twelve hundred feet or more, visibility was much improved. It was almost like flying in daylight.

Vehicles were driving very slowly down the road beneath the drone, stopping occasionally. Ant-sized figures, El Caiman's mercenaries, would scurry out of the vehicles, checking behind houses, barns, and sheds. They were obviously searching for signs of the missing carryall.

Fly steered the drone northward, away from the improved road and the vehicles. The team didn't need another encounter with El Caiman's mercs yet. She could see some lights and the outlines of some larger sheds or barns about a half mile away that looked promising.

* * *

"You can stop worrying," Vicky said soothingly. "We've got you, and you're safe now." The girl was shivering although the temperature had to be in the eighties at least. She had stopped crying, but she was still sniffling. Every few minutes she would turn her head and spit on the ground beside her. Vicky didn't need light to see that the spittle was dark with blood. "Can you talk to me?" The girl glanced up at Brad and a look of fear flashed across her bruised and battered face.

"Brad..."

"Yeah, I know. She probably doesn't want to talk in front of a man right now and I can't blame her. I'll go back up with Ving and Jared."

"Tell Pete not to come back for a bit, too, and send Jessica back here, please."

"Gotcha." Brad turned and began to cross the twenty meters of thicket, walking slowly and favoring his left side as he did so. Out of sight of Vicky, he slid his right hand beneath his nightsuit tunic and felt the scab on his side. It was still healing, and he could feel parts of it flaking off beneath his fingers as he ran them over it. The pain was manageable, but it was constant and it was sapping his strength ... not a good thing, under the circumstances. He kept walking, grimacing against the pain. That was an indulgence he couldn't permit when he reached the others. He needed them to maintain their confidence in him.

"Jess, Vicky asked if you could go back there and help her."

"Sure Brad."

"I'll come with you Jessica."

"No Charlie, let her go by herself. I think having a man present is inhibiting her."

Charlie looked chagrined. "I should have thought of that."

* * *

"She say anything yet?"

The girl looked up at Jessica. Her face really was battered. Jessica didn't think the girl's own mother would recognize her. Her clothes were expensive, even though they were torn and stained. She wore no jewelry, but Jessica could see the holes in her earlobes for earrings. Vicky had opened one of the survival blanket packets and wrapped the silver mylar covering around the girl's shoulders, presumably in case of shock. Even though it was warm and humid outside the girl was still shivering. Jessica's stomach roiled as the girl leaned over and spat on the ground next to her. The spittle was still dark with blood.

Looking at the girl's face, Jessica thought she might be reasonably attractive if she hadn't been beaten so badly. Her almond-shaped eyes and long, dark hair, her pale, white skin and chiseled features would have made her... Jessica gasped. For the first time it struck her that this might be one of the girls they were looking for.

"Chu Hua?" she burst out.

The girl shook her head slightly. "M... Meeeng," she managed to say through her shattered teeth and swollen mouth.

"Meng?" Jessica repeated in disbelief. "The daughter? Feng's daughter?" The girl nodded almost imperceptibly.

"I suspected as much," Vicky said, "but I couldn't get her to tell me her name. There aren't that many Orientals in El Salvador. We need to tell Brad what we've found out."

"Not yet, Vicky," Jessica said excitedly. She turned back to the girl. "Chu Hua? Your sister? Where is she?"

The girl's eyes filled with tears again and she tried to speak, but nothing intelligible would come out.

"Try Meng! Your sister. Where is she? Did they take her somewhere?" Meng's eyes rolled back in her head and she fainted.

"Too much," Vicky said firmly. "We pushed her too hard." *You pushed her too hard, Jess, but I'm not going to say that out loud. You're young yet and you don't know any better.* Vicky got to her feet. "Stay here with her for now. I need to tell Brad we have one of the girls we came after."

* * *

"Brad!" Vicky called in a low voice. When she had his attention, she spoke again. "The girl … she's Meng, one of the two kidnapped girls."

Brad nodded. "I was wondering about that. Too much of a coincidence, finding a badly beaten Oriental girl with a bunch of thugs of European extraction in El Salvador. I'm not a great believer in coincidence." He looked in the direction of the second Mrazor. "Did she tell you anything else?"

"She passed out when Jessica questioned her about her sister. She was obviously upset."

"I guess that leaves us right back at square one."

"Not really, Jared. She was apparently leaving the villa, which means Leclerc held on to her longer than he usually would, and the younger sister is still unaccounted for…"

"The younger sister was the prettier one," Vicky said thoughtfully. "She would be far more valuable than the older sister. It's entirely possible that he's still holding Chu Hua for some high roller with deep pockets, or maybe a special buyer might have bid on her. I think it's entirely possible she could still be in El Caiman's pseudo fortress."

"I don't know all them big words, Vicky," Ving muttered, "but I can tell you that girl is in bad shape. We can't take her with us."

"We can't leave her here, Ving. I don't know what all kinds of critters live in these mountains, but I believe I read somewhere that there are jaguar and coyotes … and that doesn't take into account the two-legged variety like we liberated her from. No, we can't leave her here."

"Brad!" Fly's excited voice floated out of the ether and into their ears. "I think I've found what you're looking for!"

THIRTEEN

Day 3, El Caiman's villa, 0247 hours

Leclerc's deep breathing exercises, usually effective, had done little to calm him. He needed a woman. The image of the delicate Chu Hua slipped effortlessly to the forefront of his brain, and he felt himself harden instantly. Just as quickly he knew she was wrong for him at the moment. She was young and innocent, and he wanted to take his time with her, savor her defloration, enjoy it. His immediate need was urgent, demanding, and brutal. Francisca's voluptuous image replaced that of the dainty Chu Hua.

Francisca was a Lenca woman, part of the community of Lenca who worked the coffee plantation that surrounded the villa. She was a full-breasted vixen who reveled in rough sex and enjoyed the luxuries of the villa that El Caiman allowed her to use when she serviced him in the way that only she could. Leclerc insisted that she bathe before their bouts, and she took inordinate pleasure in languishing in the massive tub in his bathroom, drenching herself in fragrant oils. She loved the feel of the infinitely soft lingerie that she wore for his pleasure (and that he joyfully tore from her when she resisted him, a part of the pavane that culminated in their couplings). Francisca gave as good as she got, and she relished the taste of blood ... whether his or hers was immaterial.

"Lucien, fetch Francisca! Take her to the Master Bath and stay with her until I get there. Make sure she doesn't steal anything!"

Normally this task was one Piccard would have enjoyed. Francisca was not shy, and she knew El Caiman would have Piccard's liver for breakfast if he touched her, so she taunted and teased him unmercifully when it was his turn to bring her to El Caiman's quarters. Sometimes it was hard to resist her charms and her exhibitionist streak, but this time it was not. This time Piccard's mind was elsewhere. He needed a plan, and he needed it quickly. It was only a matter of time before Leclerc learned of his duplicity—his mutiny, to put a point on it.

Crossing the man always had the same result, a slow and painful death. Piccard had witnessed enough of those to know that he would prefer not to die that way. El Caiman was a vengeful man, and he never gave up in his pursuit of those he felt had wronged him. It was entirely possible that he was going to have to kill Simon Leclerc himself.

* * *

Stefan Kubiak, a Polish national, had worked for El Caiman for years. He had helped Lucien Piccard to spring Simon Leclerc from La Santé Prison and he had stayed with the pair during those desperate days in Paris afterwards, dodging les flics and the national police. Tense times and dangerous. Days and nights of hiding, a lot of messy knife work. They had eventually stolen an old Fiat and made their way to Marseille.

Leclerc had browbeaten the captain of an ancient freighter bound for Panama that looked as if it could barely stay afloat until he had taken them aboard and smuggled them out of France. The three of them had made their way to Colón, to the entrance to the Panama Canal, before they had left the miserable freighter. In the darkest underbelly of Colón they had terrorized and extorted the criminal element until they had weapons, cash, and a vehicle capable of getting them out of the country. The gang members of Bagdad and Calor Calor were delighted to see the last of them.

Their next stop was the seaside tourist city of Tamarindo, Costa Rica, where they hijacked a shipment of cocaine belonging to Los Paveños, a Costa Rican gang that had originated in San Jose, and bound for points north, meaning the U.S. The brash, untrained Los Paveños thugs were no match for the combat-hardened Leclerc and his two companions. Leclerc had butchered the leader after the hijacking just to discourage any pursuit. It was hideous, but Kubiak was afraid to leave the company of the man already becoming known as El Caiman to the Central American underworld. Kubiak couldn't be certain, but he thought they were calling Leclerc El Caiman because of the way he left his victims scattered across the scenes of his atrocities, as if a crazed caiman had chewed and gnawed at them before dismissing them as inedible.

The three had next settled briefly in Managua while Leclerc used the proceeds from his hijackings to obtain forged documentation for them and to contact and summon former legionnaires to join them. Nicaragua is unique in Central America in that the major cartels have never established a permanent presence there, even though it is estimated that more than sixty percent of all Columbian cocaine is transshipped through the country. Groups of unaffiliated criminals known as 'tumbadores' hijack shipments for their livelihoods, often selling them back to the cartels at well under market value. The cartels treat the situation as a cost of doing business because they do not wish to stir up the Nicaraguan authorities.

The 'tumbadores' provided the inspiration for Leclerc's ambitions. He formed his new recruits into teams and began judiciously pilfering shipments bound for the Los Zetas, Sinaloa, Tijuana, and other cartels in Mexico.

It was easy, and the pickings were good, but it was not enough for Simon Leclerc. The more money he amassed the more he wanted … and money was not enough to slake his ambition. He craved power. Over men, over women, over the law itself. Nicaragua was too balanced, too determined to remain neutral.

It was Kubiak who unwittingly provided El Caiman with the final puzzle piece that showed Leclerc a place and a way he could best realize his ambitions. They had set up an ambush on Highway One in the mountains just south of Jinotepe. The small hamlet just south of Managua had a truck stop popular with transportistas coming up from Panama.

Leclerc had signaled the start of the ambush by opening up with a three-round burst from an old H&K MP5 he had taken from a hapless thug in Colón. The rounds struck the front of the lead vehicle and caused it to veer into an embankment beside the highway. Piccard had taken out the trail vehicle with a burst from his battered and worn M-16 by raking it from front to rear.

Leclerc's band had swelled to seven by this time, and they hurried down to the damaged vehicles to mop up. Kubiak had been closest to the rear vehicle, and his assignment had been to clear the

SUV and locate the drugs. When he yanked open the door, he recognized one of the wounded men inside as a former legionnaire.

"Piccard!"

"Yeah?"

"It's Richaud! Remember? From Northern Mali?" They had deployed with the 2nd Foreign Parachute Regiment (*2e Régiment étranger de parachutistes, 2e REP*) the only airborne regiment of the French Foreign Legion, on Operation Serval in 2012.

"What the hell is he doing with these low-lifes?"

"I couldn't tell you."

"Well, drag him out of there! We're not leaving anything behind." The plan was to fire the vehicles after the ambush. Leclerc didn't like loose ends, so they never left any survivors. Both Kubiak and Piccard were sticking their necks out for a former comrade in arms.

Leclerc stepped to the rear of the first vehicle, an expression of displeasure on his broad face. He was not very tolerant of deviations from his oporders, and his S.O.P. (Standard Operating Procedures) for these missions was the elimination of all the opposition forces.

“Don’t waste time on him…”

“It’s Richaud sir, from Mali!”

Leclerc’s mouth snapped shut for an instant. “Fine, bring him along, but he’s your responsibility, Kubiak. Don’t let him slow you down, though, or there will be consequences!”

“Hang on, Richaud,” Kubiak whispered. “I’ll be back for you.” He stuffed a handkerchief into the gaping wound in the fallen man’s side and then placed Richaud’s hand over it. “Keep pressure on it while I grab the product.”

Richaud lifted his head. “In … both vehicles this time … behind and under the spare,” he gasped.

Kubiak uncovered the bricks of cocaine, wrapped only in rough burlap. The cartels took care of disguising the bricks later on when they arrived in Mexico. He and the rest of the men assigned to the second vehicle quickly transferred the bricks to the trucks parked behind a stand of scrub pines twenty meters away.

Leclerc waved a hand in the air, forefinger upright, to signal their retreat.

"Wait!" Kubiak shouted. He raced to the lead vehicle, which the first team was dousing with gasoline. "Richaud says there is more." Without regard for the gas dripping from the vehicle, Kubiak ripped open the rear door of the SUV and ripped the cover panel off the spare tire. He began tossing bricks of cocaine out of the vehicle, and the others scrambled to pick them up while Leclerc stared in astonishment. And that was how Kubiak became El Caiman's number two.

* * *

Kubiak sent out motorized patrols along every possible route away from the spot where Piccard said he had found the bodies. The urgency in Piccard's voice over the radio left no doubt in his mind that El Caiman was on his ass big time. Piccard was not the kind of guy who let much of anything get to him, he was one of the coolest characters under pressure that Kubiak had ever encountered.

A detail was collecting the bodies of the dead mercenaries, wrapping them in plastic sheeting until they could be taken back to the villa. El Caiman was very careful about the way he treated his own troops when they fell in his service. The men were all hardened veterans, but Leclerc was fully aware that he could never be assured of their loyalty if he failed to respect their dead. For that reason he took pains to treat his casualties with the utmost respect.

Kubiak surveyed the scene for the fourth or fifth time. Something wasn't adding up. He had located six separate firing positions, first by expended shell casings, and, on closer inspection with a flashlight, by disturbances in the leaves and plants near the shell casings. Impressions in the hard-packed surface of the roadway indicated the presence of two wheeled vehicles, spaced about twenty meters apart, and there was something that appeared to be blood on the ground beside the right rear of the trail vehicle.

It was an odd way to set up an ambush. The positions of the shooters more closely resembled a security perimeter than an ambush; certainly it didn't look like anything he would have set up for the purpose. The coverage of the kill zone was all wrong, it just didn't make any sense. Why set up an ambush in plain view of anyone coming down the road? The shooters had used a remarkably small amount of ammunition, yet they had managed to take out nine former legionnaires, all battle-hardened veterans, apparently with only six people ... not something likely to be accomplished by amateurs.

Then there was the matter of the carryall. It was evident that the carryall had been driven at least partially off the road and that the bodies had been moved, yet the carryall was nowhere in sight. The girl was gone, too, but she was not important, just some slag El Caiman had given to the detachment to play with and then discard along the way. Diego had bragged about that, even though El Caiman and Piccard were hell on anybody discussing the details of assignments.

"Mika!" he called out. Mika, a trained tracker, came to Kubiak at a dead run and stopped, awaiting instructions. "Take Jacques and check both sides of the roadway for a hundred meters in either direction. Something is not right here."

Mika nodded and called out to Jacques. They put their heads together and then trotted off in opposite directions. Kubiak, a frown of concentration on his face, turned back to the men recovering the bodies of their comrades.

* * *

His session with Francisca was a disaster. She was at her best, but he had been so outraged that nothing she did to entice him spurred his desire. In a fit of rage, he had cursed her and dismissed her, literally kicking her out the door of his suite.

When he turned to go back into the lavishly appointed suite with its brocade covered furnishings and rich polished mahogany woods, he was almost apoplectic with rage, but out of the corner of his eye he spotted a half bottle of Courvoisier XO on his nightstand. In three great strides he was standing beside the hand carved headboard. Twisting the cork stopper, he wrenched it off the bottle. Lifting it to his lips, he drank deeply of the expensive cognac until some semblance of calm swept over him.

Carrying the bottle in one hand, he proceeded to the Master Bath so recently vacated by Francisca and stripped off his clothing. He turned the water in the glass enclosed shower on as hot as he could stand it, and then, still holding the cognac bottle in one hand, stepped under the steaming hot spray. As his skin reddened from the heat, he lifted the bottle to his lips once more, took in a mouthful of the liquor, swished it around in his mouth, then spat it into the drain.

The shower and the booze made him feel a little more centered, so he dressed quickly and made his way back down to the hardroom and his desk. He knew what needed to be done. Finding out who'd had the temerity to hijack his shipment and where they had taken it had to be his first priority.

The cell phone he normally carried was upstairs in the clothes he had taken off and thrown on the floor for the maid to pick up. Impatiently, he grabbed the landline handset and jabbed his finger at the dial pad.

"Hola! Teniente?"

The young lieutenant on the other end was a PNC watch commander, and he recognized El Caiman's voice ... and the menace it held.

"Si Senor Caiman?"

"I seem to be missing one of my vehicles. I was wondering if you might know something about that?"

"No senor, but I can find out for you if someone else in the San Salvador Department has heard anything. What kind of vehicle are you missing?" He knew very well this was serious. It was unheard of for El Caiman himself to call the station house. It was not uncommon to get a call from Senor Piccard or even Senor Kubiak, but getting one from El Caiman himself was cause for all his internal alarms to clang. He had to be very careful about how he handled this; it could be either a career maker or a career breaker. The instant he hung up it would be necessary to bump it upstairs to El Capitan Fernandes. He was so excited he never stopped to wonder why El Caiman had not called Colonel Diaz first. He grabbed a pencil from the cup on his desk and slid a yellow legal pad over to write on.

"A new black stretch carryall, one of the ones I use to transport workers around my coffee plantations. A GMC I believe. Check with Fernandes, he has a list of my farm vehicles in his desk."

Teniente Armando Solon knew very well what El Caiman used his shiny black carryalls for, and it had nothing at all to do with farm laborers. All the officers in the San Salvador Department knew to ignore them unless specifically instructed to stop one, as did the officers of the neighboring

Departments of La Libertad, San Vicente, and Cuscatlan.

"Also Teniente, be so kind as to alert my number two should you hear of any unusual activity from the former occupants of my estate. I am given to understand that there may yet be some ... ill feelings over the details of that particular ... transaction."

Solon was too scared to even smile at the oblique reference to El Caiman's seizure of the Columbian drug lord's villa. Everyone knew the story about El Caiman's ouster of the drug kingpin and the Columbian's subsequent attempt to recover it. El Caiman had obliterated the Columbian's assault force and captured the drug lord, sending his body back to Medellin ... in about thirty little boxes.

"Si Senor, I have heard nothing myself, but I will check with the other watch commanders right away."

"See that you do, Teniente." It was a command.

*   *   *

Piccard looked anxiously over his shoulder as he walked down the hallway towards the room where Chu Hua was being held captive. He knew he was taking a chance, but he couldn't help himself. The desire to see the small, helpless female was overwhelming. He wanted to help her, touch that fragile face, to comfort her ... and he had an urgent need to be her knight in shining armor. He wanted to let her know he would save her and soon.

He checked the rotating camera in the hallway outside El Caiman's suite, watching from across the hallway until it swiveled far enough that he could slip down the hallway and down to the room where Chu Hua was being held.

FOURTEEN

Day 3, San Jose Palo Grande Church, 0400 hours

The monitor showed a relatively new barn with several pieces of farm machinery in front of a dilapidated farmhouse and several ramshackle outbuildings.

"Can you zoom in a little closer on the side opening on that tractor, Fly?" Jared was bent over the monitor, his eyes close to the screen, as he tried to get a closer look at the engine compartment. He was looking for some kind of hose with the same diameter as the one he had performed the makeshift repair on.

"I'm as close as I dare, Jared. I think somebody down there's awake."

"It's no good, Brad. I'm going to have to take a closer look. From this perspective I can't get a sense of the actual diameter of the visible hoses ...

no frame of reference and I can't make a guess at the scale."

"I hate taking the chance, but if you're not sure this is going to hold I guess we've got no choice."

"Better we have to make a quick repair after a firefight with a lone farmer than when we're up to our ass in El Caiman's hostiles, Brad..."

"I don't think we're in much danger of getting in a firefight with a lone farmer. He probably hates the bastard as much as we do. Trouble is, he's probably scared to death of the man and he might rat us out as soon as he sees us. Let's get a little closer and take a better look." Brad knew from long experience that Jared was practically a ghost when it came to recons. The man was effectively a silent shadow in the night, so much so that Ving had once remarked that Jared was so slick that he could sneak up to a man, steal his radio, and leave the music there. High praise coming from Ving, who was no slouch when it came to moving undetected at night himself.

"Time for some sneakin' an' peepin'!" Ving was rubbing his hands together in anticipation, a broad smile creasing his face. The big man enjoyed this part of his profession even though he took it very seriously. He took great pride in his ability to move invisibly. It was an exceptional accomplishment for a man of his bulk.

"Okay, listen up. We get within three hundred meters and then we unass the Mrazors and proceed on foot. Jared, you and Ving go in light, sidearms only. The rest of us will take up support positions and cover you until it looks like you're clear or until you get back with a replacement hose." Brad looked up at the faces of his team. He was trying to decide who to leave at the Mrazors to watch over them and the girl. Jessica was the obvious choice, but he didn't want her to feel slighted or think that he didn't have confidence in her. The truth was that Meng was still terrified of the men, and she responded better to Jess than she did to Vicky, probably because Vicky was older. Vicky saved his ass.

"I'll hang back with the Mrazors and Meng," she said. "Somebody has to secure the vehicles." She stayed with Meng and the two ATVs at the spot Brad had designated as a rallying point. He had decided at the last moment that the one he had initially chosen from the aerial photographs back in Texas was more exposed than he had thought. Instead of three hundred meters away, they had selected a particularly thick cluster of cedar trees that offered concealment all the way to the ground. The buzzing of mosquitos near Vicky's throat mike was a constant but barely audible hum in their ears. Brad nodded in her direction.

"Let's get this show on the road, guys." Fly's voice was calm. "Nobody between you and the farmhouse right now, but there doesn't seem to be any rhyme or reason to the search pattern these creeps are using. Better stay off the roads."

The whole team shared knowing looks. Fly was bright enough and possessed a great deal of knowledge, but it was apparent she had little knowledge of the actual performance of clandestine military operations. They'd had no intention of following roads after this point. Roads were the avenue of escape when they needed to utilize the amazing speed of the Mrazors.

Brad raised his arm and waved his finger in a circle. "Saddle up!"

* * *

"Looks like a good spot up ahead for you to stop and change out the battery in the drone."

"How far, Fly?"

"About a hundred meters up and to your east about twenty, Brad. Looks like a nice thick grove and that goat trail you're on is the only path anywhere near it."

"Roger that. On our way." He heard Fly chuckle in his ear and then heard Vicky chuckle on the seat next to him over the low putter of the Mrazor's three-cylinder diesel engine. Then Vicky thrust the monitor under his nose and he could plainly see the two Mrazors crawling slowly up the steep mountain path in the moonlight from a vantage point directly above them.

The drone moved on ahead of them, lowering down until it was just within their line of sight. A tiny red light on the back of the drone body began to blink sporadically.

"We can see it just fine, Fly, douse the light."

"Just trying to help, Brad."

"You're doing fine, Fly, we just don't need the light." The light blinked one final time and then stopped. Five more torturous minutes of bouncing and bumping up the rocky path before the drone dipped down and disappeared into the forest. It had turned down a narrow footpath barely wide enough for the ATVs to negotiate, but it opened onto a small clearing covered with short grass. Brad and Ving shut the Mrazors down and the drone settled silently down to the short grass. A little door at the rear popped open.

Ving, who had stepped out of his Mrazor and walked up beside Brad in the lead one, laughed quietly, a deep rumbling sound inside his massive chest. “If a little green man climbs outta that thing I’m takin’ my ass back to Texas right now, my friend.”

Brad was barely able to keep a straight face.

“Funny, big man,” Fly drawled. “That’s the battery compartment. Which one of you yahoos has the spare batteries?”

"Got it, Fly!" Pete mumbled, stepping forward with the small battery pack in his hand, kneeling behind the drone and fumbling with the tiny catch that held the original battery in place.

"You won't have to worry about the nine volt inside for the rear light since Brad doesn't want to use it." Fly sounded irritated. No one said anything at all. Ving struggled briefly with the battery pack and then heard the replacement snap into place.

"We are mission go again," he said, wiping his hands on the seat of his trousers.

"Lead on, Fly!" Brad muttered.

The drone, its whirring motors remarkably quiet, lifted gracefully into the air and sped off over the treetops. The two Mrazors scuttled out of the clearing and back onto the trail.

The rough path began to slope steeply downward before they had traveled another hundred meters. "Start looking for another trail up to the right,"

Vicky said, looking at the monitor. "It's small, smaller than this one, a footpath really. It's going to be rough going, but it comes out right behind the barn Fly was showing us."

"You're about fifty meters from the turnoff. If you think you can find it I'm going to go ahead and take another look at that farmhouse. I can't see any of the search vehicles nearby, but I'd like to see how many people are up and about in that farmhouse." The farmhouse they had all seen in the monitor was larger than most of the houses in the small valley, definitely the property of the more prosperous residents. In the tiny agricultural community, that would normally be an indication of a larger family or the presence of hired laborers in the house.

"I think we can find it, Fly. Good thinking about checking the farmhouse again. We don't need any more surprises."

"You probably ought to try moving a little faster, Brad. According to the meteorologist's report, sunrise is only a couple hours away."

The oporder called for Team Dallas to strike El Caiman's fortress at BMNT (begin morning nautical twilight) and they were running behind schedule because of the firefight and the mechanical failure. The entire mission hinged on their ability to locate and install a stupid radiator hose. Even so, Brad did not increase their speed. He could not afford to have to turn around or go cross country.

* * *

"Go light," Brad whispered. "Sidearms only. We have you covered from here. If that farmer sees you with long guns he might panic, and we are too damned close to the villa to get caught up in another firefight."

Fly had only been able to detect the presence of a single individual moving around inside the house, but the infrared camera in the drone sensed the presence of six other adults and several small bodies as well that could have been either children or animals. Agricultural workers are notoriously early risers, and it was close enough to daylight that Brad could reasonably assume they would be up very soon. The drone hummed quietly in the air above the farmhouse, Fly keeping a weather eye on the infrared screen in front of her.

Jared and Ving separated and circled toward the barn, using their stealth to avoid detection, flitting from tree trunk to tree trunk, crawling in the taller weeds when nothing else was available. By the time they were twenty meters away, Brad could no longer see more than an occasional blip through the night vision goggles.

Jared was the first to reach the barnyard, and he low crawled over to the tractor he had spotted in the monitor. Ving reached his side a moment later, a Ruger Mark IV Tactical fitted with a suppressor in one ham-sized hand.

"Nothing even close," Jared whispered. His voice came through the earwigs as clearly as if he was murmuring in everyone's ear. "We're going to have to look at some of the other equipment."

* * *

Jesus López habitually rose an hour before his field hands did. He loved the quiet time before the dawn, and he loved to roast and grind the fresh beans from his coffee bushes, making the first pot of strong black coffee of the day. It was not a process that could be rushed, but it resulted in a heady, magnificent brew that could not be duplicated when the beans had been processed for packaging and stored.

The coffee bean is a seed of the coffee plant. It is the pit inside the red or purple fruit often called a cherry. Like ordinary cherries, coffee fruit is a so-called stone fruit. The fruits, coffee cherries or coffee berries, normally contain two stones with their flat sides together. A small percentage of the cherries, between ten and fifteen percent, bear only a single seed instead of two. These are called "peaberries". It is a superstitious belief that they have more flavor than normal coffee beans, but Jesus López was a firm believer, and he set two of his older children to sorting through the freshly picked cherries after the outer covering had been removed and separating the peaberries for his personal consumption.

The aroma wafting from the antique moka pot handed down to him from his father's father put a blissful look on his countenance as it had every morning of his adult life, and he was about to pour the first cup when he saw something out in the barnyard through his kitchen window that made his blood run cold. He stepped away from the window and hid behind the plain cotton curtains his wife had made from used flour sacks to liven up the drab kitchen. The candles that lit the kitchen flickered behind him, but he was afraid to go blow them out for fear the two men in black clothes would notice.

"Pablo," he hissed. Listening for any sound at all and afraid to leave the kitchen window, Jesus lifted a salt shaker from the counter before him and threw it against the ceiling. The top of the shaker flew of when it hit the wall and the fine white salt showered down on the kitchen floor, but Jesus was rewarded with the sound of bare feet hitting the upstairs floor.

A sleepy Pablo padded down the stairs to the kitchen.

"Senor Jesus, what is it?"

López put his finger to his lips and made a shushing noise. "Get the others, Pablo! Be quiet ... and get the guns!" he said in a stage whisper.

Pablo's eyes got wide and round and he darted back up the stairs to get the other three farmhands and the ancient rabbit-eared shotguns from the closet where they had been concealed since the end of the Salvadoran Civil war in 1992. Minutes later, there was the sound for four men coming down the stairs in a hell of a hurry. Pablo handed López a double-barreled Eibar shotgun made in the 1930s. López broke it open and checked to see that it was loaded and then snapped it shut with an authoritative click.

"Out the front door," he whispered, motioning for the four to split up, two to a side. "There are two men out by the Farmall. I do not know what they are doing, but at this time of the day you can be sure they are up to no good." All five men were terrified that they would be facing El Caiman's minions, but the tractor was a pivotal element of their success or failure, and, in their case, the difference between eating and not eating. López had a wife and children upstairs. There was no question about whether the tractor was worth fighting and even killing for, even if it meant incurring the wrath of El Caiman.

* * *

“Damnit!” Jared cursed. There was nothing else on the yard that appeared to be liquid cooled, and he looked anxiously toward the big barn itself ... and it was a long way to crawl in the bare dirt of the barnyard with no available cover.

“Got no choice, brother,” Ving whispered. “We just gonna have ta go for it and hope for the best. Brad’s got our back, and they don’t come no better than him an’ the others.”

Jared sighed and dropped to a high crawl position. “There’s gotta be a better way of makin’ a livin’, Ving.”

A rumble came from the big man’s throat and Jared realized Ving was laughing quietly.

"Go on, Jared, you know ya love this shit."

The two men took deep breaths and lit out for the barn like a pair of coyotes raiding a henhouse. They were almost to the barn when five men rushed out, shotguns pointed at them.

"*Detente o eres hombre muerto*!" (Stop or you are dead men!)

Ving reluctantly dropped the Ruger and Jared lay down on his belly, arms outstretched.

"*¡No queremos hacerte daño!*" Jared had begun taking Tex-Mex Spanish lessons from a young, attractive Mexican widow in the little town of Argyle, Texas.

"I can speak the English, gringo," López growled, leveling the double-barreled shotgun at Jared's head.

"Drop the weapons!" Brad barked as he, Pete, Charlie, and Jessica spread out from behind the tractor, weapons locked and loaded and at the ready. They had moved forward when Pete had spotted López and the field hands slipping around the sides of the barn through his night vision goggles.

López knew his shotguns were no match for the wicked looking CAR-4s and the gringos with the mean faces, and the presence of the blonde *mamacita* threw him off. He had never known El Caiman to use females for anything other than menial work or to warm his bed. He dropped his shotgun in the dirt, convinced that he was about to die. Pablo and the others reluctantly followed his lead.

López' mouth was dry as dust. He could not have mustered enough saliva to spit to save his life, but he managed to find enough courage to challenge the gringos.

"What does El Caiman want with my poor tractor? He has many such, and they are newer and better than mine."

"Are you kiddin' me?" Ving roared, recovering the Ruger and getting to his feet. He walked over and kicked the shotgun away from López' feet as Charlie and Pete moved to collect the antique weapons. "How many men does this El Caiman have with skin like this?" He lifted one massive black hand and flexed it in front of López' face. Simon Leclerc was a South African with an instinctive and powerful hatred for black people, one so strong that he had crucified the villagers in Chad for no other reasons than the color of their skin and his own perverse pleasure.

López pursed his lips as he thought hard. If these gringos did not work for El Caiman, then who? "What do the cartels want with my tractor?" He was genuinely puzzled but still very afraid.

"We don't work for no damned cartels either," Ving roared.

"Senor," Jared said calmly. "We are no friends to El Caiman or the cartels. We just need a part for our vehicle and we can be on our way. We can pay…"

López' fear dissipated. Bad men would not offer to pay, and they were rarely polite when dealing with locals. El Caiman's men were arrogant and deliberately rude, trying to provoke the farmers at every turn. More than one of his friends in the little valley had died at their hands after being ridiculed and insulted beyond the limits of their patience, their fear, or their good sense.

"You come to my farm in the middle of the night like thieves. Why should I believe you?" Puffed up with false bravado, he thought he saw a chance to make a little profit. These were not just gringos, they were *Norteamericanos. Norteamericanos* were all rich, everybody knew that. The *touristas* that came to the valley in the *autobuses de excursion* to visit the coffee plantations had money practically falling out of their *culos.* He snorted mentally. Five American dollars they gladly paid for a tin cup of coffee made from culled coffee beans that he wouldn't even allow to be sold to his buyers. Gringos were stupid when it came to money, but what could one expect from a people who lived in luxurious houses with running water inside, drove shiny cars, and had never been hungry?

He cocked his head to one side.

"What kind of part?"

Jared reached into the thigh pocket of his nightsuit and pulled out the patched six-inch length of hose and handed it to the farmer.

López thought for a moment and then turned to Pablo, the man he trusted to keep his equipment in running order.

"Pablo!" Pablo was staring, entranced, at Jessica's long, golden hair, which she had tied back in a ponytail.

"Pablo!" The younger man gave López a sheepish look.

"Yes *Senor*?"

"Put your eyes back in your head and take this gringo into the shop. Give him whatever part he needs."

"*Si Senor.*" He motioned for Jared to follow him, but he was unable to take his eyes off the slender beauty.

"Pablo!"

Reluctantly, Pablo turned away and led Jared to a small shed at the rear of the barn.

"What can you tell me about El Caiman's men?" Brad was all too familiar with the adage that one could never know too much about an enemy, and, besides, this man lived in El Caiman's shadow. He was bound to know more than even Fly's sources did.

* * *

"Got it!" Jared said triumphantly, holding up the short length of preformed semi-rigid hose. He made for the Mrazors at a brisk trot. He didn't even slow down when he passed the others, and Pete hurried after him to help with the installation.

"Senor López, we are extremely grateful for your help." Brad reached into his back pocket and carefully removed a small stack of bills from his wallet. "Thank you."

López stared in disbelief at several crisp new one-hundred-dollar bills.

"Senor, this is far too much!" He had been hoping to finagle as much as twenty American dollars from this rich *Norteamericano,* but even his avarice was not enough to justify so much money.

"You have helped us far more than you realize, my friend. Trust me, you have earned every penny of this. *Muchas Gracias*!"

* * *

"Brad! She says her sister is still in the villa!" Vicky sounded exuberant.

"Where?"

"She told me Chu Hua is being held in a fancy suite on the third floor, just down the hall from Leclerc's suite." Vicky's face went dark. "Brad, he's not going to sell her. Meng says the lecherous pervert wants her for himself."

Brad smiled grimly.

"At least we know she's still alive and where she is."

"This is going to be bad. El Caiman's command center, she says they call it the hardroom, is constantly occupied by at least three armed men, and Leclerc is often locked inside with them."

"What kind of weapons?" He looked at Meng, who pointed at the CAR-4 in Brad's hands. Then she mimed firing a weapon on full automatic.

"Well, that ain't good." He turned around and called out to Jared and Pete. "How long?"

"Done!"

"Okay! Saddle up. We ain't got much time. It's almost BMNT and we're got bigger troubles than we thought."

"What's up, Brad?" Fly's voice floated through the earwigs.

"The other sister. She's on the third floor of the villa. Leclerc's planning on keeping her as his personal toy." His voice dropped. "You getting any traffic from his communications section?"

"A lot of traffic, Brad, but it's encrypted and I haven't been able to crack it yet."

"Well keep trying, Fly. We've got to jet if we're gonna be able to pull this off."

"I don't know, Brad. I'm getting other encrypted traffic for about five clicks southeast of the villa. Something is going on and I don't like the feel of it."

"That farmer told me there's a regular barracks about five clicks from the fortress, and that's where LeClerc keeps some of his mercs. I'm more worried about the barracks in Soyapango that López told me about. He's got a lot more than enough to handle the villa security there. If he has them on alert, we could be heading into a real shitstorm."

"I think you can count on it, Brad. Maybe you should consider aborting the mission."

Brad stared at the faces of his team, one at a time. They had all gathered around to listen to his conversation with Fly, even though they could have heard it clearly through the earwigs wherever they were. Then he looked at the poor, swollen face of Meng. “No freakin’ way, Fly. We’re goin’ in.”

FIFTEEN

Day 3 EL Caiman's villa/fortress, 0457 hours

Leclerc slammed the phone down on its cradle angrily and bellowed for Piccard.

"Where the hell did he get off to?"

The radio operator picked up a pencil and scribbled furiously on a legal pad on the desk in front of him. Talking to El Caiman when he was pissed was definitely not on his list of favorite things to do. It certainly wasn't conducive to good health.

The guy watching the bank of security camera monitors busied himself by switching back and forth from array to array so that El Caiman would think he was too busy to answer. It didn't work.

"Oskar! Where is Piccard?"

Oskar Schultz, another South African expatriate and former legionnaire, turned towards the angry warlord in response. By doing so he barely missed the sight of Lucien Piccard creeping silently and swiftly down the hallway ... from the direction of the suite where Chu Hua was being held.

* * *

Piccard was very pleased with himself. Chu Hua had been frightened of him at first, but he had quickly reassured her and then just as quickly had given her hope by promising to get her out of the villa and away from El Caiman. The young girl had clung to him gratefully as he'd explained to her that he had a plan. When she pressed him for details, he deflected her questions without raising any suspicion in her young mind, but it had taken every ounce of his ingenuity to do so.

He had not told her that she would not be returning to her home and her father, nor had he told her of his desire for her. She would come to accept that in time because he would be comforting and gentle with her—and because he was certain he could make her totally dependent on him. It would just require infinite patience.

* * *

"Lucien!" Leclerc roared as Piccard entered the hardroom. "Where have you been?"

"Checking the inside sentries." It was stretching the truth, but it was a lie he could at least partially substantiate.

Leclerc waved a hand dismissively.

"Call Boucher at the barracks in Soyapango and Ortega in San Salvador. Tell them to mobilize and get here as soon as possible. Alert the others as well. I am convinced there is going to be another attempt made by the Medellin to take back my villa."

Piccard stared at Leclerc in amazement. The Medellin hadn't been a force since the early '90s, which is why he had gotten away with confiscating the estate in the first place. If they'd still been in their prime, Simon Leclerc and all of his men would have long since been obliterated. The Medellin had been cruel, ruthless bastards willing to kill anything or anyone, and they had feared nothing. Eliminating an upstart like Leclerc would have been child's play when they were in their glory days. Leclerc was an adept leader, but he would have needed an entire brigade of the Legion to withstand the former power of the Medellin. Now that cartel was a bad joke, and Piccard had carefully steered his boss away from offending *Los Zetas,* the *Sinaloa,* the *Jalisco New Generation,* or the *Juarez* cartels.

He was making his break with El Caiman in the nick of time. Leclerc was losing it. He obeyed his orders immediately anyway, his mind focused on retrieving the drugs ... and the cash, from the 'missing' carryall. It was time to bail on El Caiman. The man was losing his mind.

* * *

"Boucher is calling the men back to the barracks in Soyapango." The men didn't actually live in the barracks, it was more of an assembly area. The San Salvador complement used the Soyapango Barracks as well, but they were not called out as often. El Caiman used former legionnaires as his cadre. The rest of his mercenaries were drawn from former military types from all over the world but mostly from Central and Latin America. "The Santa Tecla and San Marcos contingents have been placed on standby." The two contingents were rarely used. Privately, Piccard considered them a tribute to Simon Leclerc's tremendous ego. They were well armed, of course, but they were not as well screened or well trained as the primaries. Piccard didn't trust them.

"How long?" Leclerc boomed.

"Boucher says any time now, Ortega thinks he can be here in force in a couple of hours." Both men knew the time estimates were optimistic. Living in El Salvador, some of the customs and habits of the region tended to rub off on the legionnaires. El Salvadorans were anything but punctual, and all of those men were at home asleep. Leclerc grunted.

"Every man, Lucien! I want every man who isn't working in the villa outside and on the ground!"

"Yes sir, but we don't have enough of the ATVs to go around." Leclerc's brows beetled and his face grew mottled with rage.

"They have feet, don't they, Lucien? Let them walk! This is not like you... Do I have to think of everything?" *Get a grip on yourself. Lucien is the best number two you have ever had and this is not like him at all. He is not a man who rattles easily; he has proven himself time and again.*

Leclerc's face smoothed out and he regarded his old comrade in arms. Piccard was frantically barking orders into a cell phone. In all the years Leclerc had known him he had never seen the man panic, not even in Northern Mali when the brigade commander had arrested them both and put them in irons for having a little fun with some insignificant peasants.

He is hiding something... What is it? With Boucher's contingent and the ones Ortega can muster, I have enough men to hold off anything the Medellin can throw at me. I know they aren't as strong as they were years ago, and I know Lucien has been steering me away from the others' shipments... I don't think he knows I know, but I do. Arrogant bastards, but Lucien is right. I am not strong enough to stand up to them yet, especially Los Zetas. *I will be soon though! Very soon those sons of whores will grovel at my feet. The government... Pah! The government is interested only in maintaining the status quo.*

They will not be a factor as long as I do not bring my war to El Salvador.

He had already purchased substantial acreage near El Capulin, in Honduras, with the intent to build a training camp there that would put "*La Ferme* (The Farm)" to shame. "*La Ferme*" was where all legionnaires began their five-year contracts, training with the 4th Foreign Infantry Regiment near Castelnaudary, a small country town in Southern France. In addition to physical training comparable to that of U.S. Navy SEALs, recruits were required to learn to speak French. It was one of the toughest military courses on Earth, and it lasted for four months.

He had planned to send Piccard to run the camp as soon as the barracks and support buildings were completed; the project was being executed in total secrecy and neither Piccard nor Kubiak were privy to the details. He intended to raise a full brigade with which he could challenge even *Los Zetas.* It was an ambitious project that he'd had in mind since those early days in Colon, and it was very close to coming to fruition ... but first he had to deal with this ... this ... affront to his reputation and his dignity.

* * *

Piccard's head was spinning with the effort of organizing the rest of the mercs at the fortress into two-man foot patrols. The watch commander, a former sergeant in the *2e REP,* had to be alerted, and together they'd tried to make adjustments to the routes of the ATVs. The task had proved difficult, as they did not want the motorized patrols to clash with the foot patrols, but they needed the routes to overlap in order to provide a tighter security net. It would require very accurate timing to pull off ... too much to let the original patrol routes stand.

"Pull the motorized patrols. Set them all on foot and set it up so they have to meet at both ends of their posts."

The sergeant was not certain that the roving sentries should walk their post in pairs because it would leave large stretches of ground uncovered for a considerable length of time, but he could plainly see that Piccard was in no mood to listen. Sometimes it was better to just say, "Yes sir," and let things go, and this appeared to be one of those times.

"Yes sir!"

* * *

Piccard did not go directly back to the hardroom. The problem of how to spirit Chu Hua out of the villa and then retrieve the coke and the cash from the carryall was looming large in the front of his mind. Time was running short. Kubiak was as good as anyone he'd ever worked with, and it was only a matter of time before he or one of the trackers managed to track down the missing carryall. Piccard cursed himself for not concealing it better, even though he was well aware that he had done the best he could with the time he'd had at his disposal.

Strolling through the villa on the pretext of checking the guards—and incidentally ensuring that they had not divulged that the carryall had been located and concealed—Lucien whittled down his options one by one until he was left with two possible alternatives. His best estimate was that neither alternative offered more than a 50/50 chance of success, but that did not bother him. He had performed combat missions with lesser chances of success, but this time he alone would reap the benefits. Life on a tropical island with the delectable Chu Hua at his beck and call—he never for a moment considered that she might not be a willing participant in his fantasies—was a goal worthy of the risk even if it meant killing his long-time friend and mentor.

Killing Simon Leclerc would be distasteful, but Lucien knew that the man would never stop looking for him once the theft of the narcotics and cash was discovered. El Caiman had founded his reputation on his merciless and unforgiving nature. Simon Leclerc would have to die. The only thing that remained to decide was the how, when, and where.

As Lucien roamed the three floors of the villa, stopping at random checkpoints to verify that the guards were in place and alert, a plan began to slowly take shape in his mind. Killing El Caiman was not the only problem he faced. Getting out of the villa was going to be a problem as well. If his assassination plan worked the way he intended it to, the guards would not be aware of El Caiman's death when Lucien left with Chu Hua. There would be no time for challenges and explanations, that much was certain. His departure would need to be as rapid and unremarkable as possible. Another complication that he had no immediate solution for.

* * *

"Done!" Lucien exclaimed, closing the door to the hardroom behind him. He watched Oskar Shultz lean forward and flip a switch on his console and heard the three heavy, electronically operated deadbolt latches in the door slide home with a quiet but solid thunk behind him. El Caiman did not acknowledge him immediately, he was hunched over his desk, toying with a bronze letter opener shaped like a dagger, deep in thought. Suddenly, he raised the letter opener and slammed it into the thick wood surface of the desktop, leaving it quivering there as he turned to face Piccard.

"What is done, Lucien? Tell me exactly."

Piccard felt his insides turn to ice. *Could he know? Had one of the mercs told him about finding the carryall?* His mouth was dry and it felt as if his vocal cords were paralyzed, but with great effort, somehow he managed to talk in an almost normal tone of voice.

"We ... I ... changed the motorized patrols to foot patrols and issued a challenge and password each pair of sentries has to exchange at the limits of their posts." He took a deep breath, his courage returning bit by bit. "There was some good-natured bitching and moaning, but the men understood why the change was necessary."

Leclerc frowned. "They are getting soft, Lucien. None of them would have dared to gripe within hearing of even a *caporal* in their Legion days."

"Those days are long past," Piccard said softly. "Life here is not as tough as it was in those days."

Leclerc's eyes narrowed and his face took on a smug, self-satisfied look that sent chills racing up and down Piccard's spine.

"Those days may be coming back, Lucien. I have plans, big plans. Someday very soon we will be having a long discussion about that, eh? The time has come for us to talk about expanding our reach and our capabilities ... and increasing the size of our force."

He tried to restrain himself, but Lucien's eyes gave away his incredulity. Leclerc held up a hand.

"I know, I know. The men have gotten sloppy, especially Ortega's mob—and that is what they are Lucien, make no mistake about it." He sat back in his desk chair and clasped his hands behind his head. "It is time we started talking in terms of platoons, companies, battalions ... perhaps even a regiment."

Piccard's eyes widened. The man was insane. Even the apathetic government of El Salvador would never permit a fully trained military organization on their soil. They would be forced by the major powers to take action, or the powers themselves would intervene. Madness!

Leclerc didn't seem to notice Piccard's astonishment. He sat up abruptly and reached for the carved wooden box on his desktop and gently removed a genuine hand-rolled Cuban cigar then fastidiously clipped the end of it with a golden cutter. Setting the cutter down, he lifted a matching gold lighter from its tray and carefully lit the tip, rotating the cigar over the flame until precisely half an inch of gray ash was showing. Only then did he lift the cigar to his lips and take a puff.

"We will talk more about this later, Lucien. At the moment, we have a more pressing problem to deal with, and it requires our full attention. I have reason to believe the Medellin are behind this hijacking, and I think the hijacking itself is a prelude to another attempt to take my villa away from me."

It was plain that Lucien had to finalize his plans and fast. Killing Leclerc had become an absolute necessity. He fondled the hilt of his Arkansas Toothpick absently, trying to decide if the time was right. He glanced at the three men on duty in the hardroom and calculated the odds against him. They were only armed with sidearms, but still, the chance of a successful assassination attempt and escape was slim. He needed to lessen the odds a little. An idea popped into his head.

"Oskar!"

Shultz looked up from his monitor console, one eyebrow raised in question.

"I saw some wires hanging loose from one of the rotating cameras outside the kitchen door when I was making my rounds a few minutes ago. Why don't you let me take over the monitor station while you go check it out for me?"

Shultz turned to the bank of monitors and flicked a couple of buttons.

"Everything looks okay from here. I think it's probably—"

Leclerc bit down hard on his cigar and jabbed a finger toward the grizzled man at the monitor.

"There! That is what I am talking about, Lucien." He glowered at Shultz. "You would never have questioned an order from a superior when you were an honest legionnaire, Oskar. Hell, you would have been flogged! Do as you're told! Lucien is perfectly capable of watching your television sets!"

Leclerc leaned back in his chair, chomping angrily on his cigar. "Sloppy. All of you have grown fat and sloppy. I have been far too lenient with you. Very soon now things are going to change." His jaw worked angrily as the stunned Shultz stared at his leader. "Go!" Leclerc roared, half rising from his chair. "Are you deaf as well as stupid? Has it occurred to you that the *Merde-rempli* Medellin may have penetrated our perimeter and tampered with the cameras?" Still furious, he crushed the partially smoked cigar in the ashtray on his desk and spun around to face the wall. He had lost his temper in front of his men, a trait he found abhorrent in any leader, and he knew he had to get himself back under control.

Lucien gestured for Shultz to move, and the older man scooted for the door. Reaching down to the familiar console, Lucien opened the electronic locks and watched the man hurry out of the room. Closing the locks once the door had shut, Lucien glanced at the other two men, who were trying very hard to appear busy. The odds against his success had been lessened by a third, but he needed something else, a distraction of some kind.

He focused on the monitors, desperately racking his brain for some way to create a distraction for the other two men.

SIXTEEN

Day 3, Outside El Caiman's estate, 0512 hours

On the move from the farmer's barn to the objective, Jared's sharp eyes had spotted a clump of greenery on his monitor located on the far side of the crest among the coffee bushes that seemed out of place, and he had pointed it out to Brad. Fly had taken the drone down as low as she thought she could and zoomed in on the cluster. It was a good spot for an LP/OP (Listening Post/Observation Post), but if that was its purpose, its builders had done a masterful job of camouflaging it.

"Keep an eye on it, Jared. I can't tell if it's occupied or not, but we're not going to chance it. Belay the planned ORP (Objective Rally Point) location and I'll designate a new one en route." Fly's technology was providing them a means of communicating and gathering situational intelligence that was little short of amazing.

"Where was this shit when we were in Fallujah?" Ving muttered under his breath. The Second Battle of Fallujah, known as Operation Phantom Fury, had been the bloodiest confrontation of the entire Iraq War and the most intense urban warfare involving the Marines since the 1968 Battle of Hue City in Vietnam. Ving had been awarded the Navy Cross for his act of heroism in that battle. Brad had just been happy to come out of it with his ass in one piece.

"The Army probably had it."

Fly's voice crackled over the earwigs.

"They did not! In 2004, this was still *Star Wars* stuff. Just a daydream on some geek's wish list."

"There!" Vicky pointed to a thick grove of pine trees at the military crest of the hill overlooking El

Caiman's villa. Brad slowed the Mrazor to a crawl in order to minimize the noise from the exhaust.

"Perfect!" he muttered. He raised his left hand and made a circle in the air, then lowered it, his fingers and thumb extended and joined and pointed toward the grove—the signal to designate the ORP. Fly's drone had shown them the roving foot patrols between the foot of the hill and the villa, and Brad had timed their arrival so that the sentries would be out of earshot.

The two Mrazors slipped into the grove and the team silently offloaded and took up positions in a three-hundred-sixty-degree perimeter with the practiced ease of a Force Recon squad. Vicky remained at the center with Brad and Meng. Brad began to quickly check over his equipment. Vicky touched her throat mike.

"What do you think you're doing?" she whispered.

Brad touched the disc on his own throat.

"I'm not comfortable sitting here while Jared and Ving check out that clump. I'm going with them," he whispered back. He started to rise, but even as he got to his feet he winced involuntarily from the pain of the half healed wound in his side.

"The hell you are, Brad," she retorted hotly.

"Vicky, don't fight me on this. I'm responsible for them!"

"You go down there and you're liable to get them killed, Brad. You're in no condition for sneaking around in the dark and you know it. How's that responsible?"

She was right and he knew it, and he hated it. If there was an LP/OP in that clump there would be knife work... There were too damned many mercs roving the grounds and this mission was already risky enough as it was. Alerting El Caiman to their presence too soon would get all of them killed. The success of the mission was critically dependent on stealth, surprise, and shock. He nodded his agreement to Vicky and settled back down beside the Mrazor. It rankled him to do it, but he gave the hand signal to Jared and Ving to move out.

The two men left the grove as silently as wraiths, disappearing into the shadows almost instantly.

"They really are good at that, aren't they?" Vicky whispered.

"The best." Brad settled back to watch the scene from the viewpoint of the drone, high above them. The resolution on the camera lens was remarkable, and the light gathering ability of the lens was unearthly. Even so, Jared and Ving were so good at their craft that Brad heard Fly speaking in his ears after a few seconds.

"Lost 'em. Switching to infrared."

The red spots on the monitor were moving at a snail's pace toward the clump, but there were no red spots visible in the clump.

"Doesn't look like there's anyone in there," Brad breathed.

"Don't count your chickens just yet, hotshot. Infrared is only accurate if those critters haven't shielded their position… Those little mylar survival blankets and six inches of dirt will screw with the sensitivity of this little gadget." Fly sounded intense. "Gotcha!" she cackled as a narrow red blip flashed on the screen. Something in the cluster had moved and her 'gadget' had caught it. "There's at least one critter in there, guys. North side."

Jessica was rear security on the perimeter, and she was a little irritated about it, but it was better than babysitting Meng. Even so, she couldn't hear anything and she couldn't see anything. She opened her mouth to speak and glanced over at Charlie some twenty meters from her position. Charlie put his index finger to his lips in a shushing motion and her mouth snapped shut audibly, which earned her a dirty look from Pete. She wanted to get moving again. What she really wanted was to give El Caiman a chance to shoot at her so she could end his miserable life. All she needed was a chance.

* * *

Ving could see okay with the night vision goggles, but he couldn't see the interior of the LP/OP at all, and there was not a hint of the presence Fly had reported. He was apprehensive, but he knew what he had to do. He intended to stay as close to the right side of the position as possible, keeping whoever was in there between him and Jared. That rangy Texan was quick as a mongoose, and a man could shave with that Kabar he carried. Ving had been shot before, and he didn't like it, but he hated getting cut with a passion that bordered on the psychotic. He shrugged his massive shoulders and fingered his own Kabar. He was waiting for the grunt from Jared that they'd agreed on as the signal to go.

* * *

Jared heard every word Fly was saying, and he was on the north side of the grove. Ving was circling around to the right, but there was no time to worry about him... Fly had reported sighting somebody on the north side and that was what he had to concentrate on. He was within five meters of the cluster, and he could see the dim outline of what looked a lot like a revetted foxhole. The night vision goggles were excellent, but the shadowy interior of the position was murky and indistinct. He was going to have to go in blind, which meant he would have to move with the speed of a striking rattler. He was afraid, but he had long before learned that courage wasn't about the absence of fear—only an idiot felt no fear. Courage was about mastering your fear and doing something that scared the shit out of you anyway. The only thing he was truly worried about was Ving. It would be fighting blind in close quarters and he had no idea how much room was actually in the revetment. Ving was a big man, and Jared hoped he wouldn't hurt his friend. No time to worry. He eased the big Kabar out of its sheath on his harness, grunted, and sprang.

* * *

He hated being set out on a listening post. It was boring and Louis, his partner, had been snacking on *kimchi* for the last hour. The stench of garlic permeated the revetted position and was making him gag. He had no idea why anyone would even put that nasty fermented cabbage in their mouth. Louis seemed to love the stuff. A glance at his watch told him they still had two more hours before they were relieved. *Merde!*

A large, rawboned hand clamped around his mouth at the same time his body was slammed into Louis'. Before he could even react he felt the tip of a large knife press against his chest just below his xiphoid process protrusion and then felt a sharp pain as the blade angled upward and into his heart. Then everything went black.

* * *

"That was quick!" Fly's tone was evidence of her relief. She had sat through many missions in her years at NSA, but somehow this one was hitting harder than the others. For years she had watched operatives that she'd never met performing missions that she had helped create at a distance from intelligence gathered by someone other than herself. Not only was this mission one of intense personal interest, one might even call it an obsession, she had gotten to know and admire this intrepid group of people. A bond she'd never known in government service was growing rapidly inside her. She turned her attention back to piloting the drone. She still had work to do.

* * *

"For some reason the patrols have been dismounted, Brad. All of them are walking now and there are more of them."

"Any kind of pattern to the patrols? Without being able to hear those ATVs coming it's going to be a lot tougher to break that perimeter."

"Got you covered! Got the drone up to twelve hundred feet and I'm scoping out the patrols. Looks like two-man teams but they're running a pattern that doesn't make any sense."

"What do you mean?"

"They're walking in pairs, about four hundred meters apart. The way they're walking it looks like it will take about twenty minutes to cover their sector, but... Wait a minute. These guys are meeting at the end of their post and jabbering about something. Jesus, Brad, they're leaving about eight hundred meters uncovered while they jawjack."

"Then we need to time our penetration for when the two posts meet."

"Exactly, but you don't have a lot of time before the sun comes up. You'd better hope this pattern holds."

Brad turned to Ving, who was swabbing a long scratch on his upper arm with an alcohol swab from his First Aid pouch.

"Gettin' careless in your old age?"

"Nah. Not me." Ving inclined his head toward Jared, who was wiping down the blade of his Kabar. "That countrified clown din't watch what he was doin'."

Jared looked up with a grin.

"Cain't see you in the dark if you ain't smilin', Ving," he drawled.

"Sheeeit!"

"Enough with the small talk, everybody listen up. We're cutting it close and we were already running behind the time schedule. Did everybody catch what Fly said about the patrols?" Everyone gave him a thumbs up.

"Good! As long as the pattern holds the sentries should meet again just below the LP/OP in about fifteen minutes. I want to take all four of them by surprise at once, just the way you two"—he glanced at Ving and Jared—"did a few minutes ago." He cocked his head to one side and thought for a second. "There isn't much in the way of concealment down there, so we're going to need a quiet distraction. Any ideas?"

"I know exactly what to do to keep those boys' attention without alerting their supervisors," Vicky said, standing up and unzipping her nightsuit to a point just above her navel.

"So do I," Jessica whispered hoarsely, "and you know those guys are starved for blondes down here." She unzipped her own nightsuit, a little lower than Vicky had. Then she removed the hair band from her long, blonde ponytail and shook it out. Her hair billowed out like a halo, and then she cocked her hip to one side suggestively. Brad glanced at Charlie first, who shrugged and grinned sheepishly, and then at Vicky, who nodded her approval with a slight motion of her head.

"Okay Jess, you got it. I want you to conceal yourself until you get as close as you can get to their meeting point. When you hear them talking, close with them and get their attention. When you are sure all of them are focused on you, I want you to pull your hair back behind your ears. That will be the signal for the takedown. Got it?"

Jessica acknowledged him with a bob of her head. "At last...

Something to do besides perimeter security or babysitting."

* * *

The four sentries approached each other lackadaisically, and it was plain to see that they weren't taking their duties seriously. Jessica could plainly hear their challenge and password. As the four men stood laughing and talking quietly, she stepped forward from behind the cedar tree she had concealed herself behind with her arms spread wide and wearing what she hoped was a look of distress on her face.

"Oh! Thank God! I thought I would never find somebody to help me!" she wailed. All four men spun around, their weapons at the ready, and for a moment her terror was unfeigned. It looked like they were going to shoot her and her heart jumped into her throat as the index finger of the man closest to her squeezed down on the trigger of his H&K MP7.

Jared leaped out, Kabar in hand, but Jessica could see that he was too far away to reach the gunman in time. Her survival instincts kicked in instinctively and she clawed for the ground, scrabbling for cover though she knew in her heart it was hopeless. She cringed, expecting to feel the impact of the 4.6x30 mm rounds at any second.

She didn't see it happen, but a hole appeared in the bridge of the gunman's nose as the silenced Ruger spat out two rounds, the second catching the man in his right eye before ricocheting around in his brain pan and turning it to mush. Jared's knife struck home beneath the second man's rib cage just as Ving and Charlie silently took down the two remaining sentries at the same time. Jessica looked up from her prone position to see an anxious Pete standing above her with his own Kabar in his hand.

"You okay, Jess?"

"Uh, yeah," she said faintly. She glanced up to see Brad walking toward her, the Ruger Mark IV Tactical dangling limply from his right hand. She noticed for the first time that he was favoring his side, where Hamdani had stabbed him.

* * *

"Okay, Fly, you got that floor plan of the house handy?"

"Sure thing. Just a sec." The floor plans of the villa appeared on all the individual monitors.

Brad thrust his monitor in front of Meng, who was sitting wide-eyed beside Vicky.

"Can you show me where they are keeping your sister?" Meng nodded wordlessly and pointed at the diagram of the third floor. "Third floor, Fly!" The screen blinked and suddenly filled with an enlarged diagram of the third floor. There were two large suites and a hallway, and Meng pointed at the back suite. "Who sleeps in this one?" Brad asked, pointing at the suite toward the front of the hallway.

"El Caiman!" The words came out garbled because of her bruised and swollen lips, but everybody understood her.

"I know this is a lot to ask, Fly, but do you think we could get one of these tiny drones inside the villa?"

"I can't guarantee it without you getting close enough to launch it. You know the battery life on those things is half an hour, right?"

"Yeah."

"If you want to chance it, we can give it a shot. I can't be sure they don't have jamming capabilities, there's a lot of white noise coming from the villa. I'm not sure what's going on." There was a brief period of silence before Fly came back. "Can't help you on this end, Brad. I have no idea. You may want to consider aborting the mission… I've never seen an electronic signature like this before. It's a new one on me."

The eyes of every member of the team were on him, but Brad was carefully weighing his options. *Improvise, adapt, overcome!* They'd never had the benefit of the kind of technology that Fly had provided them on this mission before. A snippet from a lecture he'd attended on Human Intelligence for Special Operators at MARSOC (Marine Special Operations School) in Camp Lejeune, North Carolina ran through his mind.

The starchy, grizzled old master gunnery sergeant had stood before the class in utilities waiting for the class to be seated. He didn't really have to wait because the volunteers were all gung ho and really wanted to attend the course, but he took his time, which ensured that all of the students were sitting on the edge of their seats waiting breathlessly for the old school Marine to shower some of his wisdom on them.

"You're going to learn about all kinds of gadgets for intelligence gathering in this class today." He

grimaced. "Mostly they work, but I'm here to tell you something and I want you to write it down." He paused for effect, staring down every member of the class. "There ain't no magical thingamabob, no doohickey, no electrical widget, that can replace these." He pointed, using exaggerated arm and finger movements, at his brain, his eyes, and his ears. "That's where it's at, gentlemen. Even when you get those mountains of information, and you will get tons of it, from those gadgets, you still have to use what the Good Lord give ya ta make somethin' useful out of it and ya still haveta make your own decisions about what ta do with it."

Aborting the mission was never an option. *Improvise, adapt, overcome!*

"Give an aerial of the approach to the villa one more time, Fly, and then see if you can get an infrared image of the villa itself. I need to know how many personnel are inside right now and I need to have an idea of where they are. Can you put the thermal image on the monitor?"

"Can do, Brad." There were several minutes of silence as she worked.

"Lock and load!" Brad ordered tersely. "As soon as we get updated visuals on the approaches we move out. I want to get as close as we can without being detected so we can try to launch that littlest drone, but if we can't we're going in anyway."

Jared and Ving uncased the deadly little American-180s, a submachine gun developed in the 1960s that fired .22 LR cartridges from a pan magazine at a rate of 1200 rounds per minute. The guns, when fired, made a sound like a swarm of angry bees, and the volume of fire was more than sufficient to send even experienced troops diving for cover. The standard pan magazines accommodated one hundred and eighty .22 LR cartridges, but Jared had fitted them with aftermarket magazines that carried two hundred and seventy-five rounds and flash suppressors to help conceal the location from which the guns were being fired. Short of carrying an actual mini-gun, the American 180s were the most effective suppressive fire weapons any of them had ever used. Both men carried several of the pan magazines in shoulder bags.

Jessica retrieved a duffel bag of fragmentation grenades from the rack on the rear of the second Mrazor and began to distribute them, while Pete shouldered a rucksack containing forty pounds of C-4. The remote detonators he carried in a claymore bag draped across his chest. The oporder called for multiple M112 charges to be placed in and around the villa to be set off more as a distraction while they exfiltrated with Chu Hua than to destroy. The M112 is a rectangular block of Composition C-4 about two inches wide by one and one half inches thick and eleven inches long, weighing one and a quarter pounds. The M112 is wrapped in an olive-color Mylar-film container with a pressure-sensitive adhesive tape on one side so that they can be affixed to a vertical surface. Brad carried several small breaching charges in a claymore bag on his chest to take down the entry doors to the villa and to the hardroom.

"Got it!" Their personal monitors blinked and split into two screens, one showing a video of the approach to the villa from their position, the other half showing a live thermal image of the villa through the drone camera lens. "Just tap the side you want to look at and you can zoom in with your touch screen. When you want the other image back, just tap the screen twice."

Vicky left Meng, who seemed to be recovering from her fear of the men, and peered over Brad's shoulder as he scoped out the terrain between their position and the villa.

"That row of coffee bushes runs parallel to the front of the villa all the way up to this fold here," Brad said, tapping the screen with his forefinger.

He cursed as the screen changed to the thermal image. "Not used to this damned thing!"

"Just tap it again and it will go back to the one you were looking at, Brad." Fly's voice sounded suspiciously like she was holding back laughter, which she was.

Brad grimaced and tapped the screen. The image showed that there were no personnel in the cultivated area.

"We have enough battery life to leave the drone aloft until we get closer to the villa?"

"Plenty left in this pack, Brad … at least another hour's worth."

"Good! Keep an eye on the thermal image and let me know if you spot a pattern or any kind of movement in the house while we're moving."

"Roger that!"

Brad turned to Meng.

"Are you willing to come with us to the villa to get your sister? Are you able?" Meng managed a nod, even though Brad could see that it cost her. He made up his mind.

"Vicky, bring her along. We can't leave her here, she's helpless by herself. We're just going to have to suck it up and take her with us."

Ving, who had been watching and listening a little apprehensively, offered a suggestion.

"You think maybe we should try to take the Mrazors in a little closer, Brad? Their speed would be a real asset when all them assholes start shootin' at us, and they're damned sure going to do that when we start blowin' stuff up."

Brad considered the suggestion for a moment. Ving was right about needing to get out in a hurry, and they *were* going to be handicapped. Meng was in no condition to move fast and there was no telling what condition Chu Hua was going to be in. It was a chess problem. Which was he going to sacrifice—speed or surprise? The decision was difficult, but he made up his mind and committed to his decision.

"We stick with the original plan. Vicky, you and Meng stay tight on my six. Move out!"

The team formed up, Jared on point and Ving taking rear security so that their firepower could cover the whole team on the move. Brad signaled for them to move out.

* * *

Piccard was idly flipping through the screens, waiting for Oskar to return, his mind fully occupied with trying to figure a way out of the fix he was in. Out of the corner of his eye he caught some movement on one of the screens covering an area where no guards were supposed to be. He flicked the button in front of him rapidly, going back to the cam where he had seen the movement.

Five men and three women, one of whom he barely recognized as Meng, one of the two abductees, were creeping along one of the rows of coffee bushes toward the villa. Somehow they had managed to circumvent the sentries on the north side. The man in the lead was tall and rawboned, and he was cradling a light submachine gun in a businesslike manner that suggested he was very proficient with it. Piccard knew a warrior when he saw one, and all of these men were warriors. The two women were a mystery to him, but the men looked downright lethal.

Glancing up at Leclerc and the other two men still in the room, he saw that none of them had noticed the intruders. The idea came to him just that fast. He leaned forward as calmly as he could and shut the camera down, as well as the other cameras between the first one and the villa. It was just the distraction he needed.

SEVENTEEN

Day 3, The Fortress. 0541 hours

Oskar had called in, reporting that he'd been unable to locate the loose wiring, but Piccard had shut him down, insisting that he must have given the wrong location by mistake. According to his calculations, by the time Shultz got to the new location to check it out, the assault would already have begun. There wasn't a great deal of time left before sunrise and the intruders moved like men who knew their business.

Tension flooded his body as he anxiously watched the other two men in the hardroom. They had noticed nothing and none of the sentry teams had reported anything out of the way yet. That couldn't last long. Leclerc was busy lighting another cigar, and there was a silver brandy flask on the desk beside the cigar lighter. Leclerc was losing his shit.

He would never have considered taking a drink before combat in the old days with the Legion.

Piccard broke out in a sweat. He would have to make his move, and he would have to make it soon.

*   *   *

It didn't make sense to Fly. What kind of lunatic would protect an LP/OP from being spotted by thermal imaging and leave his communications nerve center unshielded?

She shook her head back to the thermal imaging screen. The guards inside the villa were not moving around like the outside guards. She thought that was a little odd, too, but a lot of what she was seeing didn't make sense. The suite Brad had told her Chu Hua was in on the third floor was occupied by a lone red blip, and a larger blip was standing outside the door. The suite Meng had identified as being the private quarters of Leclerc was empty, but there was someone or something she could not identify on the *outside* of the suite that appeared to be clinging to the outer wall. What the *hell*?

There was no way she could move the drone off station. Brad and the others were approaching the villa and she knew it was critical to maintain the thermal image of the inside of the villa at this point ... but she would keep an eye on that figure scaling the wall outside El Caiman's suite just in case.

* * *

Francisca had tucked the rough osnaburg fabric of her skirt into the rope belt at her waist and kicked off her rough leather sandals before beginning her climb up the stone wall of the three-story villa. El Caiman had lost interest in her. She had tried every fancy trick she had learned over the years to entice him, even the ones she despised, but he had cursed her and then kicked her as she left his suite.

She had no intention of ever coming back to this pig's suite to entertain him again. For two years she had answered every one of his calls and satisfied even his most perverted demands, often having to lose several days of work because his lust for rough sex left her unable to perform for her other 'friends' or even work the coffee plantation. To make matters worse, he hadn't even paid her or given her a gift for tonight's humiliation. Never again! She was going to make him pay for this ... and she knew exactly where he kept his valuables too.

El Caiman had never bothered to hide his valuables from her, he didn't consider her to be a threat. He was in for a rude awakening. Tonight, she knew, he would not go back to his suite. When he was in a rage, he always went to the special room where he kept his radios and electrical toys, and he drank. No one would be in his private suite, guards weren't allowed there except for that

Piccard *arrastrarse*, and he was busy supervising all these extra men.

Her hand slipped and one of her fingernails curled back painfully, but she didn't cry out. She dug her calloused heels into the rough stone and continued to climb, blood seeping from her injured nail. There was gold in El Caiman's suite, and jewelry, and there was a man in a back alley in San Salvador who would pay well without asking any questions.

* * *

Anatoly Kitzak and Roli Czernik were usually paired with other partners because of their propensity to goof off when they were supposed to be working. The *caporal* supervising the surprise early morning detail was still sleepy and did not catch the slip-up. No sooner had he posted the two men than they were at it again.

"What in the name of God is this shit all about?"

Roli laughed. "I heard El Caiman is in another of his moods. Emile said Francisca was mad as the devil when she left last night."

"Ah, he didn't get any! No wonder he's in a pissy mood."

"Yeah, and we end up having to pay for it by walking a stupid make-work security shift because he didn't get his ashes hauled!"

"The *caporal* said the Medellin hijacked one of the shipments last night and that they were coming to take El Caiman's villa for themselves!"

Roli rolled his eyes. "The Medellin*! Los Pepes* finished the last of those bastards in 2007." *Los Pepes*, their name derived from the Spanish phrase *"Perseguidos por Pablo Escobar"* ("Persecuted by Pablo Escobar"*)*, was a short-lived vigilante group formed by the enemies of Pablo Escobar. They fought a small-scale war against the Medellín cartel in the early 1990s, which ended in 1993 after Escobar's death. "They haven't been a threat to anybody since '93, and as to this being El Caiman's villa, hell, he 'confiscated' this place from a damned Columbian drug lord!"

Anatoly looked confused. He had heard the barracks gossip but had written it off as idle chatter. Gossip was always present on easy gigs like this one; the easier the tour the more fanciful the rumors. "So there is no threat?"

Roli turned to look in the direction the *caporal* had walked off in and could no longer see the man.

"Hell no! El Caiman is losing it, man, I think he's getting psycho or something. This shit is all in his head. Come on, I know a place we can go where the cameras can't see us. We can have a smoke." He tapped a pocket on his vest. "*And* I have a flask of *Tíc Táck* in my pocket!" *Tíc Táck,* an unaged sugar cane liquor, is the unofficial national drink of El Salvador.

"I don't know..." Anatoly looked around as if he expected someone to be watching them. He had no way of knowing that Piccard had just turned off the cameras in their sector. "What about the carryall, Roli?"

"Tempest in a teapot," Roli said, waving his hand in a dismissive gesture. "This is El Salvador! There are gangs a plenty out there, and you know they are crazy enough to take on El Caiman. These people are hungry and scared, but they are getting bolder. This was a sweet gig when we started, but things are getting flaky around the edges, you know?" He stuck the unlit cigarette in his mouth, where it danced crazily as he continued to speak. "It's getting time to think about moving on ... another job." He clapped Anatoly on the back "Come on. It'll be starting to get light anytime now, and we need to talk about this over a drink. What do you say?" He turned and walked down toward a row of coffee bushes without looking back to see if Anatoly was following him. There was a drainpipe from the irrigation system about fifty meters down that first row, and it led to a natural fold that transected the front lawn of the villa. The fold was deep enough to conceal the light from his cigarette from the cameras.

* * *

Despite the narrow window of time they had before daylight, Brad resisted the urge to hurry. Only three minutes into the final movement toward the villa it had become painfully obvious that Vicky was not going to be able to provide all the assistance Meng needed to walk, even though the girl was trying gamely to keep up. Brad hesitated only a second before motioning for Charlie to come forward to assist Vicky.

Jessica had proven herself to be cool under pressure and to have excellent judgement, but she was still the youngest member of Team Dallas, and she still tended to feel like Brad was being overprotective of her at times, which he had to admit he was doing on occasion. She was, after all, his younger cousin. He had to make a better effort to treat her the same as the others.

Turning back to Jared, he gave the signal to move out, pumping his fist in the air twice and pointing forward. Jared slunk forward, his American 180 at the ready, his pace steady, although a bit slower this time to accommodate Meng's unsteady progress.

They had moved perhaps another hundred meters before Jared raised his fist in the halt sign and motioned all of them to the ground. Instantly the team responded, going to the prone position. Jared crawled back to where Brad was lying, their faces together. Jared pointed to his eyes, then raised two fingers and then pointed to the front. He mimed circling around and coming from behind, and then drew his forefinger across his throat. Brad nodded and then made as if to go with the rangy Texan, but Jared put a hand on his shoulder and shook his head no. Then he made a V with his forefinger and middle finger and started moving toward Ving, but not before Brad gave him a one-finger salute. He was in considerable pain, but he knew Jared was right.

* * *

Roli shouldered his way roughly through the last two rows of coffee bushes making no particular effort to maintain noise discipline. He was convinced that the whole Medellin scare was nothing more than what he considered to be El Caiman's growing paranoia and monumental ego. Anatoly followed him, cursing in his native Russian instead of the French he had been forced to adopt as the limber branches of the bushes whipped back and caught him in the face.

When they went through the last row, both men crouched down low and walked down into the fold in the earth that served as a drainage ditch and then sat down cross-legged in the deepest part.

Roli cupped his hands around a plastic butane lighter and flicked the striker wheel, touching the resulting flame to the tip of his unfiltered *Gitanes* cigarette. He inhaled deeply and then handed the pack and the lighter to Anatoly. As Anatoly flicked the lighter's wheel, a massive black hand closed over Roli's mouth and there was a searing pain in his neck. Then there was nothing at all.

* * *

The pain was getting worse, and he could tell that the wound had reopened. The bleeding wasn't bad yet, but he could feel it, warm and sticky and starting to soak into his nightsuit. He didn't dare stop to put a compress on it, Vicky would have a fit and there was no time left... The first rays of the sun would come peeking over the horizon soon and he'd wanted to make their exfiltration under cover of darkness for obvious reasons. As it was, they were going to be stretching into Civil Twilight when they made their exit. Three hundred meters back to the Mrazors was going to be a stretch for them with Meng in tow, and he didn't have a clue as to what shape Chu Hua would be in when they got her. He refused to think of his own pain. It was gut check time.

EIGHTEEN

Day 3, El Caiman's Villa, 0558 hours

Fly had kept the drone aloft to keep an eye on the thermal imaging, but she had focused on the villa itself and not the outside. There were more guards present outside than they'd counted earlier.

Shit, we need some sort of distraction or Pete is never going to be able to get close enough to place his charges! Brad cursed himself for not taking this situation into consideration during the planning phase of the oporder. He clenched his fists, concentrating, but the throbbing pain in his side was fogging his brain. The blood was beginning to flow down the leg of his nightsuit and he knew he was going to have to think of something quickly.

* * *

Jared assessed the situation, knowing Brad was doing the same, but he'd known the man long enough to know there was something wrong. He wouldn't let himself show it, but Brad was hurting bad. Something had to break, and quick, or the mission was going to go south. He rolled over onto his side and felt the roll of electrical tape in his thigh pocket, and the inspiration hit him like a thunderbolt. Rummaging in his back pocket, he found and pulled out a bandanna.

"Quick!" He hissed. "Give me a couple more bandanas!" Nobody asked why, they just tugged out the OD green cravat triangular muslin bandages, commonly referred to as 'drive-on rags' that they all used for bandanas and passed them to him.

When he had three, he wrapped them tightly around the flash suppressor on his American 180 and then covered those with the remains of the roll of electrical tape. It wasn't perfect, but it would muffle the sound of the rounds exiting the muzzle a little, and that was all he needed. He signaled his intentions to Pete and then crawled up on the back lip of the ditch and sighted in on the gatehouse.

"Go!" he whispered hoarsely to Pete. He didn't wait to see if the big man had moved, he opened fire on the gatehouse, three-round bursts, walking them up to the glass windows of the little stone building and causing instant pandemonium. The gatehouse guards began to fire wildly out the shattered windows with their unsuppressed weapons, causing some surprised sentries along the front perimeter to rush toward the gatehouse. Jared sent a couple of bursts into the running men and then ducked. *It had worked! The guards were firing at each other, and the roving sentries were rushing toward the gatehouse!*

* * *

Brad opened his eyes to see Pete running in a crouch, the heavy rucksack on his back not slowing him in the least, toward the front of the villa.

"Go!" he barked, no longer worried about being silent. The yells and the gunshots behind him were loud enough that no one was going to hear him. Jared's weapon going off behind him startled him, but it had taken no time at all for him to realize what Jared had done and why. He got to his feet and waved everyone forward.

* * *

Pete rushed for the electrical service room on the south side of the villa, Charlie hot on his tail providing cover. The plans showed a standard door, something Pete considered foolish of Leclerc but fortunate for him.

They came under fire as they rounded the side of the house; a pair of roving sentries coming from one of the outbuildings shouted at them and let off long, wild bursts from their submachine pistols. Pete fired on the run, but Charlie calmly dropped to one knee, took aim, and squeezed off two three-round bursts from his Car-4, dropping both sentries.

Pete never slowed down, throwing his shoulder into the solid core wood door and splintering the frame. Inside, while Charlie stood in the doorway keeping an eye out for more sentries, he shrugged off his rucksack and lifted out four blocks of C-4. Peeling the film off the pressure sensitive adhesive tape, he pressed the block across the thick line going into the bottom of the service box. He took a pair of non-metallic pliers from a pouch on his web belt and used the sharp end of the handle to bore a hole in the block of C-4 then took a timed detonator out of the claymore bag on his chest, setting it for five minutes. Five minutes would give him time to set a few more charges around the outside of the villa. The little electrical gizmos that sent the charges to the detonators were one of the little toys Fly had given them. She had pointed out that the radio controlled detonators were too risky to use around El Caiman's communications system.

He glanced around the room trying to locate the power feed from a backup generator, but there were so many thick cables on the walls and none of them went into the power service.

"Shit!" He pulled out four more blocks of C-4 and rigged them together with short lengths of det cord, crimped a booster onto the end of one of the gizmos, and secured the blocks in a fan pattern beneath the service box. "We need to get outta here, kid," he muttered. "In a little less than five minutes, anything within fifty feet a this place is gonna be toast!" He shoved Charlie out of the way and raced for the next spot he and Brad had selected for a charge, which was, ironically, beneath the camera Shultz had been sent out to check earlier.

Pete was tamping the C-4 around its detonator when he heard Charlie let loose two more three-round bursts from his Car-4, but he didn't turn around. He had come to trust Charlie almost as much as he did Brad, Ving, and Jared. "Go!" he shouted as he set the gizmo to four minutes.

* * *

The pain was getting worse by the second, but Brad stoically ignored it as he pressed the door charges over where he thought the hinges should be on the inside. Then he wrapped a thin strip of the plastic explosive he had fashioned back in Texas before they had left the ranch around the massive door plate and handle and hurriedly stuffed a detonator into the soft clay-like substance. He backed away from the door parallel to the stone wall until he was safely out of range of the blast and then plugged the clacker into the wires and screamed, "Fire in the hole!"

He pressed the clacker handle and the charges exploded, sending stone, plaster, and wood shooting out onto the manicured lawn. Jared was through the door before the dust had settled, closely followed by Ving and Jessica. He could hear the American 180s buzzing along with the sharp cracks of Jessica's CAR-4. Vicky, half carrying Meng, brushed up against him as the two women limped past. Vicky blanched and stopped in her tracks.

"You're bleeding!" she accused. There was a streak of dark red on the back of her hand.

"No time! Go!"

Vicky flashed him a dirty look and then maneuvered Meng through the hole where the door had been moments before. Brad followed behind them, his CAR-4 at the ready.

He moved his face close to the girl's.

"How do we get to where Chu Hua is?" he shouted over the buzzing of the American 180s. Meng, her eyes wide with fear, pointed to a staircase at the end of the foyer. Brad scraped against the wall as he swept past Vicky and the girl, leaving a red streak on the off-white paint.

"Damn him!" Vicky exploded, furious. She turned and hurried down the hall as quickly as she could. Half carrying Meng, she could not unsling the CAR-4 from her shoulder, so she fumbled the Beretta 92FS from its holster on her web belt and switched it to her left hand. Meng was almost her own size, and it took all Vicky's strength to keep the girl upright. She briefly considered depositing Meng on one of the brocaded sofas in the massive living room to their right, but she was immediately ashamed of the thought. Gritting her teeth, she headed down the foyer to the stairway behind Jared, Ving, and Brad.

They managed the first flight of stairs to the second floor, but Vicky was straining to get Meng that far. A shot rang out and a bullet thudded into the wall by Vicky's head. She let go of Meng and dropped to one knee, snapping off a double tap into the belly of a mean looking man dressed all in black and wearing the golden logo of El Caiman on his sleeve. He was writhing on the floor in agony, but his weapon was still in his hands. Vicky left Meng leaning against the wall while she went to him and kicked the weapon away. She checked quickly to see if he was carrying a sidearm, and, seeing none, she hurried back to Meng.

"Come on," she said. "Brad will be down in a second with your sister." *If she's still there,* she added silently to herself. She couldn't remember how many of the red figures were on the third floor, but the buzzing of the American 180s was all but continuous as well as the sharp bark of Brad's CAR-4. The rattle of the H&Ks was deafening. Grimly, Vicky holstered the Beretta and unslung her own CAR-4, tapping the heel of the magazine before leaning down to take Meng's arm over her shoulder. She was turned around and could not remember which way the hardroom was. That was where Brad and the others would be headed. At that moment she felt the villa shudder and then heard a monstrous boom. The building went dark and she heard Fly screaming a warning in her ears that sent ice water rushing through her heart.

*   *   *

The two men on the third floor had fought viciously, and Ving had felt several bullets tug at his nightsuit, but so far he hadn't been hit. A monstrous boom made the floor beneath his feet wobble, and he saw Brad stumble and fall. Fly was screaming a warning into their earwigs, but it didn't really register until a hidden door at the end of the hallway opened and black-clad men began to pour into the broad hallway.

Jared, a half step in front of him, shouted a warning and lit up the hallway with a hail of bullets. Ving had no time to check on Brad, his life depended on getting his pan magazine switched before Jared's ran out of ammo. He knelt down and snatched another magazine from his pouch in one smooth motion, removed the old mag and attached the other, clicking it home just as Jared's mag ran out.

The infrared images had told them that there were only two sentries on the third floor, but there had been no way for them to know that the building had been modified since El Caiman had taken over the property. A hidden staircase had allowed a half dozen men to access the third floor when they'd heard Brad breach the front door.

Ving jumped to his feet, already firing as Jared dropped to reload. The stench of cordite filled the hallway as Ving finished shredding the bodies of the men who'd come through the door with his American 180.

"Smokeless powder my ass!" Jared growled, waving his hand in front of him in a vain attempt to clear the air so he could see better.

"Get the girl!" Ving roared, kneeling down once more to check on Brad. He saw that his closest friend was trying to struggle to a sitting position, and he reached out to help him sit up. Brad started to get to his feet and Ving realized that his hand was covered with blood.

Jared disappeared into the door to the second suite and emerged a second later with a gorgeous young Oriental.

"Brad, where you hit, man?" Ving wiped his hand off on the expensive carpet beneath his knees.

"I'm not hit, Ving. It's the knife wound from Borneo, it's reopened." Ving's eyes widened in mixed fury and admiration.

"You damned fool! Why didn't you say something? You shouldn't have even come on this mission! What were you thinkin'?" He reached forward to grab his comrade's shoulder, but Brad shrugged the big hand off.

"I can make it, Ving." He shook his head to clear it as he slowly stood up. "Did Jared get the girl?"

"Got her!" Jared said, dragging the girl up to them. "Crap man, what happened?"

"He reopened that stab wound an' didn't tell anybody, that's what happened!" Ving said angrily.

"Focus people! We can deal with what I did or should have done later. Right now, we need to get Vicky and Meng and get the hell out of here."

"We still gotta get the man, Brad. It don't sit right with me to come all this way an' not take that crazy bastard back with us. That dude needs to sit in ADMAX for the rest of his born days!" Ving was clearly agitated. The United States Penitentiary, Administrative Maximum Facility (ADMAX) is a federal prison in Florence, Colorado that provides a higher level of custody than a maximum security prison. It is often referred to as the Alcatraz of the Rockies.

"Too bad we can't just off him and get the hell out of here," Jared grumped. "Pete ain't used all that C-4 yet. Forty pounds woulda made a bigger bang than that."

"Go!" Brad pointed to the stairwell. "This place is going to be crawling with mercs any second now."

* * *

Vicky steadied Meng and breathed a sigh of relief when Brad, Ving, and Jared returned with Chu Hua in tow.

"Meng!" Chu Hua tore loose from Jared's grip and raced to embrace her battered sister.

"No time!" Brad barked, taking Meng by the shoulder. "We—"

Jared's American 180 opened up and two men down the second floor hallway fell to the floor.

"We gotta go, Brad!"

Leaning against the wall, Brad led them down the hallway to the hardroom.

* * *

"We both shoulda brought them damned little 180s," Pete groused. He and Charlie had placed the last of the C-4 and were busy fighting off El Caiman's mercs from behind a flower bed retaining wall. They were running low on ammo for their CAR-4s and the mercs were still coming. He glanced down at his watch. "Any second now, Charlie, this place is gonna start comin' apart."

Charlie smiled grimly. It couldn't happen soon enough to suit him. He aimed at a spot where he had just seen the head of a merc duck down behind a concrete fountain and was rewarded when the idiot's head popped back into sight. He squeezed off a round. "Got him!"

Pete was staring wistfully at the H&K lying beside one of the dead mercs only a few feet away when the first explosion shook the ground. He'd been expecting it, but he was not expecting to see a curvaceous Latina wearing a rough osnaburg dress tucked up around her waist land on the soft grass next to him.

"What the...?"

The woman was stunned, but she got to her feet unsteadily. She had something wrapped up in the folds of the skirt. Despite the pandemonium around him, Pete couldn't help but notice that she had long, shapely legs and wasn't wearing any panties. Then he looked up to see an open window on the third floor and understood that she had fallen when his first charge had detonated.

"You okay?"

Francisca looked up at the white giant but she couldn't understand what he was saying. She got a tighter grip on the folds of her skirt, filled with booty from El Caiman's room, and began to race for the coffee fields. Screw El Caiman! The bottoms of her bare feet flashed in the twilight as she ran.

Pete didn't have time to waste on the running woman. He dove for the H&K and used the dead merc's body as cover while he felt for spare magazines. Charlie was still shooting, though there seemed to be fewer mercs around. The next of the charges detonated and the lights on the grounds blinked two or three times and then went off. Despite the massive charge he had left in the power room, the lights inside the villa stayed on.

NINETEEN

Day 3, The Fortress, 0612 hours

The explosion rattled everything in the hardroom, and El Caiman jerked in his chair, chewing the ragged stump of the cigar and spilling his cognac.

"*Medellin!*" he bellowed. He turned his head to Piccard, still at the console. "How did this happen? Why were they not seen on the cameras? *Merde!*" Not waiting for a response, his face mottled with rage, he turned back to his desk and snatched his phone off its cradle, dialing Boucher's cell number.

"*Où sont mes hommes*?" (Where are my men?) he screamed into the handset. Whatever answer he got infuriated him further and he pushed the receiver button down several times and began to scream into the handset, apparently at the guards in the gatehouse. Even while he was screaming he was pushing the button that would sound the klaxon mounted on a pole outside the power room.

The klaxon did not come on. He slammed the handset down in the cradle so hard that it broke in half and then grabbed one of three handheld radios from a charger on his desk.

There was no time to check on the other two men in the room. Piccard took a deep breath and stepped from behind the console, slipping his Arkansas Toothpick from its scabbard and closed with the raging Leclerc. He had left his Beretta on the console where he had put it earlier, and this situation called for knife work anyway. He was aiming for the spot where the ribs met the spine, his dagger angled upward toward the heart, but at that instant another explosion rocked the house and the dagger entered straight into Leclerc's back.

Leclerc's spine arched backwards against the offending steel even as he stumbled forward onto his desk before collapsing to the floor.

Piccard spun around, reaching for his sidearm, expecting to see the other two men coming after him, but an explosion from the hardroom entrance blew the door off its hinges and onto the floor.

* * *

Brad fought off nausea as he leaned against the heavy steel hardroom door. His fingers fumbled with the soft plastic explosive charges and placed the detonators, but he stubbornly refused to let Ving or Jared help.

Charlie arrived in the hallway behind Jared and Ving, out of breath and with Pete right behind him. He saw Brad struggling, but one glance at Ving's broad face warned him not to say anything.

"Fire in the hole!" Brad cried, throwing himself to one side away from the blast area.

The team hugged the walls as a cloud of dust and plaster showered them before the door blew inward and hit the floor with a resounding crash.

A split second later, Jared and Ving tossed flash-bang grenades inside the room. The flash was brilliant, and the explosion, while not powerful, was loud as hell. They rushed into the room spraying fire from the 180s indiscriminately. Neither of them was much concerned with capturing El Caiman alive at that point.

Two of the men inside the hardroom tried to return fire with sidearms, but their resistance was short-lived. When the dust settled and Jared and Ving stopped firing, there were three men inside lying sprawled on the floor. Jared knelt beside one of the men and checked his pulse while Ving checked the other. When Charlie checked the third man, he detected a weak pulse.

"Over here!" he called out. "This one's alive!"

Jared raced to the man lying face down by a fancy polished mahogany desk.

"We didn't get this one," Jared said. "This guy's been stabbed in the back. Thready pulse and probably in shock." He was stripping open his First Aid pouch. Ripping open the man's shirt, he slapped a compress over the ugly wound and applied pressure to it to try to stop the bleeding and Jessica squatted down beside him to help. She began swabbing the blood from the skin around the compress.

"Could be worse. Doesn't appear to have struck any vital organs and the bleeding is not that bad." His voice was calm as he worked, as if he wasn't in the middle of an estate crawling with hostile mercenaries bent on killing anything that moved and explosions going off in rapid succession. Jessica leaned forward and turned the man's head to one side so she could get a look at a nasty bump on his forehead that was bleeding.

She let go of his head as soon as she recognized him from the photos Fly had given them.

"It's him!" She spat out the words. "Leclerc."

*   *   *

Chu Hua stepped away from Vicky and her sister when she heard Jessica call out Leclerc's name and stepped inside the hardroom.

"El Caiman?" she said hesitantly, walking with tiny, mincing steps to where Leclerc lay. Her face was an inscrutable mask.

"That's him, honey," Jessica said in disgust. She had dropped the alcohol swabs she'd been using to clean up his blood, unwilling to touch him anymore. She had an almost overpowering urge to just shoot the bastard, but she fought it off. Brad had made it clear there was not to be a repetition of her behavior with Guzman in Peru. Her own stomach turned when she remembered what she had done to him.

Chu Hua was under no such constraint. She lashed out with her foot, catching Leclerc on the chin.

"Bastard!" she screamed, and kicked him again. Jessica grabbed her from behind and pulled her away from Leclerc. "Let me go!" Chu Hua twisted out of Jessica's grip and kicked Leclerc again. "Bastard!" she was crying. "That's for my sister!" She kicked again before Jessica and Charlie could restrain her. "He killed Jorge," she sobbed. Jessica wrapped her arms around the girl and held her close. She glanced at Brad, who promptly looked away.

"Take her back out to her sister," he said quietly. The girl really was a beauty and so young. It was painful to see her heartbreak, and somehow it was harder to see her hatred of the sorry bastard on the floor. No child, and that was what she was, a child, should be made to feel the way she did. God only knew what else Leclerc had put her through.

* * *

Lucien Piccard shuddered, claustrophobic, inside the concealed closet El Caiman had secretly constructed inside his hardroom. The closet was supposed to be known only to Leclerc, but Piccard knew everything that went on in the villa. He had raced to the closet and shut himself inside when the door had been blown off its hinges. He could hear everything going on in the hardroom. *Americans!* He felt his heart leap into his throat when he heard Chu Hua's voice. What were they doing with her? Her sister? Why did they bring her sister back to the villa?

It hit him then. These definitely were the ones who had hit the carryall, but they weren't here for revenge or the drugs. They were here to recover the two girls! He fought back a rising panic. They were going to take Chu Hua! All his dreams and plans were about to go up in smoke unless he could stop them somehow ... but all he had was his beloved dagger. His Beretta was lying on the console of the bank of monitors.

He leaned forward and pressed his ear against the wall. He needed to know how many of them there were. He could not let them take Chu Hua, his plans had come too far along, and apparently Leclerc was not dead. He had risked everything and not only would it all have been for nothing if they took Chu Hua, but Leclerc would come after him. There wasn't a prison made that he believed could contain Leclerc, and he knew how vindictive the crazy *connard* was.

* * *

"Heads up, Brad! Incoming personnel! Looks like three trucks headed your way, about five clicks out."

He didn't ask how many men were in the trucks. At that range the display would only show a large, red blob in the back of the trucks. There was no time left to lose.

"Pete! How much time is left before your other charges blow?"

Pete glanced down at his watch.

"The last ones are set to go off in eight more minutes."

"Fly, where are the outer sentries concentrated?"

"Most of them are out front, Brad. Not sure why, but most of them skirted around toward the gatehouse when that first explosion went off. Most of the ones that were left after the bunkhouse blew up went to the woods just south of the villa. There aren't a whole lot of them left, maybe ten or fifteen." There had been more than thirty men on sentry duty, and there was a trace of admiration in her voice.

"Jared, have you and Ving got enough ammo left in those 180s to make it out to that closest shed where they parked the ATVs?"

"No sweat, we can handle it."

"Pete, retrieve a couple of blocks of C-4 and bring them back here. I've got an idea of how to slow down those guys in the trucks when they come in after us. Jared, you and Ving try to get a couple of those ATVs so we can get Meng and Leclerc back to the Mrazors. We're gonna have to move fast. She isn't up to it and he is out of it."

Vicky thought, *Neither are you,* but she didn't say a word. She did, however, exchange a knowing glance with Ving, who gave a slight nod of understanding. A couple of the ATVs they had seen on the monitors were John Deere Gator models with truck beds behind them. They would take those ... and they would trash the others.

* * *

Charlie spoke up.

"Maybe I should go with them, Brad."

Brad was too weary and weak to argue. Speed was a necessity, and time was running out on them. There was still work to do before they could take the two girls and Leclerc out the back door and he needed just a minute to gather his strength. The reopened wound was taking more out of him than he'd thought. He took a knee.

"Jess, I don't care how you do it, but get him ready to transport. We're out of time." He sounded tired, even to himself.

"I'll start moving Meng and Chu Hua to the back door," Vicky said. "Pete can help you get Leclerc." She was worried about him, but she knew him well enough to know that it was not the time to show him she was. She and Chu Hua began to herd the injured Meng back out into the hallway.

* * *

Piccard panicked. Chu Hua was leaving with the Americans and if he didn't do something immediately she would be lost to him forever. He screwed up his courage and then opened the concealed door just a fraction of an inch.

Leclerc was lying prone on the floor, just as Piccard had left him except that now there was a breathtakingly beautiful blonde woman trying to put a bandage over his wound. A large, muscular man was between Piccard and Leclerc, facing away from the closet. There was no one else in the room. It was now or never.

Drawing his still bloody Arkansas Toothpick from its scabbard, he slammed the closet door open and threw himself across the space between himself and the kneeling man.

* * *

Jessica glanced up at the sudden noise and screamed when she saw a menacing looking man dressed in black with El Caiman's emblem on his sleeve come out of a bare wall with a wicked looking dagger in his hand.

Brad whipped around, barely in time to grab the wrist of his assailant. There was white-hot agony in his side as he struggled to keep the razor-sharp tip from reaching his chest. The impetus of the man's leap sent Brad tumbling backwards, and the point of the dagger inched ever closer despite Brad finally managing to get both hands wrapped around the man's wrist.

The two men were rolling around on the floor, and Jessica was afraid to fire her pistol for fear of hitting Brad. The Glock 17 was too light to do much damage as a club, and her eyes darted frantically around the room, searching for anything heavy enough to use as a club. She spotted a nearly empty brandy bottle on top of an expensive looking polished mahogany desk and lunged for it, leaving her patient still bleeding on the floor. Wrapping her fingers around the neck of the bottle, she spun around and brought it down full force on the back of the assailant's head. The bottle made contact with a sickening clunking sound and then shattered, raining glass shards down on Brad's face. The assailant slumped straight down on top of Brad, and the dagger dropped to the floor.

"What's happening?" Fly's voice floated over the earwigs.

"Jess just saved my ass," Brad gasped, giving his cousin a weak grin. With a grunt, he shoved his attacker's body off of his and slowly got to his feet.

"Is he okay, Jessica?" Vicky's voice sounded forced.

"I'm okay." He took a couple of breaths.

"Trucks passing the gatehouse, Brad!" Fly's voice was shrill.

"We got rides!" Ving's voice rang out in the earwigs. "Come on down!" The last sentence sounded like something from a popular daytime game show.

TWENTY

Day 3, The Fortress, Daybreak

Pete ran into the hardroom, four blocks of C-4 in his big hands, out of breath and sweating.

“What the hell...” He was panting. “I got back as quick as I could. You okay, Brad?”

“Give me the C-4, Pete, and throw that sack of shit over your shoulder. We gotta get outta here.” Brad pointed at Leclerc.

“What do we do about him? Jessica asked, pointing at the unconscious black-clad assailant.

“Leave him,” Brad said dismissively. “He’s not important. Let’s go.” With a little more pep than he felt, Brad limped painfully down the hallway to the staircase and then down the first floor hallway to the rear door. He stopped just inside the doorway and placed the four blocks of C-4 against the wall at floor level and carefully attached the detonator wires to the detonators. Carefully covering the blocks and wires with a doormat, he payed out the detonator wire from a short coil in his pocket.

Ving rolled up in a nearly new Gator and skidded to a stop.

"Come on, Brad!"

Brad waved Pete and Jessica toward the idling Gator.

"Get 'em out of the blast area, Ving!" He held up the clacker in his hand. As soon as Pete laid Leclerc down on the bed of the Gator and climbed up beside him, Jessica hopped in the front seat beside Ving. Gravel spurted from the wheels as Ving accelerated out of the way. Jared and Charlie sped by a moment later as flames started licking around the outside of the garage where the ATVs had been stored, and then a great gout of flame shot through the roof of the building, accompanied by a thunderclap as the gasoline tanks inside exploded.

Shaking his ears to try to regain his hearing, Brad crouched down in the lee of a wing wall coming off the west side of the house near the back door. He waited patiently until the first two mercs passed through the house and out the back door before squeezing the clacker and setting off the explosive. Dropping the clacker on the ground, he hopped toward the parked Gators without waiting to check the results of his trap.

He didn't make it all the way to the Gators… Charlie slammed his Gator into reverse and almost backed over him, skidding to a halt just inches away from Brad.

"Go!" Brad gasped, holding his hand over the bloody fabric of his nightsuit. Wearily, he twisted in the seat and leveled his CAR-4 in the general direction of the villa.

As soon as they cleared the north side of the villa, Brad knew he had guessed wrong. The replacements had not come through the house after all. Boucher had deployed the main body, the last two trucks, to the north side of the villa because it was the most likely avenue of escape given the disposition of the surviving mercenaries.

The Gators were both slower and noisier than the Mrazors, and they began to draw fire before Jared, carrying Vicky, Meng, and Chu Hua, broke the cover of the fold in the earth they had used to approach the villa. Cursing, Vicky grabbed Jared's American 180 and began to return fire as Jared reached back with one hand to force Meng's head down. Chu Hua, understanding the situation, covered her sister's body with her own.

Ving cut the wheel hard left on his Gator, which was jouncing wildly because of the unbalanced load caused by Pete and Leclerc on the tail end, and then covered his face to keep the coffee bush limbs from whipping him as they passed through the first and second rows of the bushes. Skidding wildly, he made a hard right just inside the second row, heading for the spot where they'd left the Mrazors.

"They're in the tree line south of us," Jessica screamed into her throat mike. She scrabbled for Ving's 180, but the Gator was bouncing around so bad that she couldn't get it into position to fire. They were still a hundred meters from the Mrazors.

"Oh crap!"

"What is it, Fly?" Brad barked into his mike.

"I think they've figured out where you're headed! One of the trucks just backed out onto the road and it's headed up towards the LP/OP."

"Give her all she's got!" Brad yelled to Charlie, who already had his accelerator pressed to the floorboard. The Gators topped out at about forty-five miles per hour, considerably slower than the Mrazors. The truck had further to go, but it was faster. It was a race, and Brad didn't know if they could win it.

* * *

Gustav Boucher was growling orders into his handheld radio, trying in vain to control the contingent of troops he had brought from Soyapango. He had ordered three squads to the north side of the grounds where the coffee plantation butted up to the lush, manicured grounds of the estate, but he'd heard Rudy Kilmer, one of his more experienced squad leaders, issue a counter order sending a third of his personnel north along the roadway. It irritated him, but he trusted the former *caporal* implicitly. He would not have issued the counter order without a reason he could justify.

Boucher entered the blasted front door of the villa, looking around in disbelief. It looked as if a company of regular army infantry had come through on a rampage. The walls, those still standing anyway, were pockmarked with bullet holes. The walls were blackened from explosions and fire, and most of the furniture was riddled with holes. Someone had set a regular hailstorm of bullets loose inside the house.

The staircase was relatively untouched … if you didn't count the cracks and fissures in the plaster. He made his way to the second floor and turned to his right, headed for El Caiman's hardroom. He wasn't sure he wanted to see what was there, but if anyone was left in charge, that's where they would be.

The heavy steel hardroom door had been blasted off its hinges and was lying on the floor inside. The two men manning the monitors and alarm systems were sprawled awkwardly in death over their consoles. Boucher turned to the right and saw Lucien Piccard, his old friend and El Caiman's number two, trying weakly to get to his feet, his hand on the back of his head. He ran over to the injured man.

"Lucien! What happened?"

Piccard stared down at the huge pool of blood on the floor where Leclerc had lain. He needed to be very careful what he said next.

"I don't know, Gustav. All I can tell you for sure is that El Caiman shouted something about the Medellin coming to take back the villa. Then everything got crazy for a while... He made me call you and Ortega up. I wasn't sure what he was so excited about, but you know him. When El Caiman shouts, we all do what he says. Life is easier that way."

"Okay, but what about ... all this?" Boucher's hand waved around the destruction in the room.

"I don't really know, Gustav. We got no alert from the alarms or from the cams. I was on the monitor console because Shultz had to go make some repairs on an outside camera. The next thing I know, the door blew up and El Caiman was lying on the floor here bleeding pretty badly."

"Is he all right?"

Piccard shook his head slowly.

"I don't know, Gustav. He looked bad… I thought he was dead, but when I got up just now, he was gone."

"So what do we do now, Lucien? With El Caiman missing, you are in command until we find him."

Boucher's words electrified him. *"You are in command until we find him."* The Americans had taken Chu Hua, and his dreams were shattered. They had obviously taken Leclerc as well—*leaving him in command.*

"Call everyone in unless they are directly engaged, Gustav. We need to reorganize and consolidate, and then we need to start cleaning this place up. El Caiman will be pissed if we haven't gotten started by the time he gets back." Piccard truly believed that Leclerc would return, if he lived. It might take years, but no prison could hold him for long.

In the meantime, *he,* Lucien Piccard, was *in charge.* The cash and drugs in the carryall were small potatoes compared to the riches just within his grasp now. Chu Hua was fast fading from his memory. When a man commanded untold riches, beautiful women flocked around him like moths around a candle flame ... or he could just buy one. Hell, he had all of El Salvador and several of the girl markets at hand. He could buy a dozen. Perhaps Leclerc's idea of expanding was not so far-fetched after all. He stood up, dusted himself off, and headed for El Caiman's suite. No telling what surprises he might find there.

* * *

Daylight had broken, and the Mrazors were in sight. Jared's Gator was sputtering, slowing down. He couldn't tell if it was a bad fuel filter, a clogged line, or something more esoteric. The gas gauge read full. They were going to have to hoof it the last fifty yards or so unless he could nurse it a little closer.

Charlie was right on Jared's tail, and Brad was firing his CAR-4 at the oncoming truck, still some hundred meters or so away. Several men were firing at them from the truck bed, but their fire was not very accurate because of the jostling and unsteady firing platform. Brad seriously doubted that his own fire was effective for the same reason, but he hoped that it served as suppressive. Jessica had obviously run out of ammo for the 180, the angry buzzing sound of the .22LR cartridges had stopped.

"Go!" Charlie shouted, waving Jared on with one hand while the other tried to hold the steering wheel steady as the Gator bucked and plunged over the rough terrain. Brad turned to look at the Gator in front of them and saw that Jared had slowed to a crawl.

"Push him, Charlie," he shouted, seeing that Jared was having trouble.

Charlie did as he was told, nudging Jared's Gator with the brush guard on the front of the ATV. The two tangled together inextricably, but it didn't matter. They reached the Mrazors just as Pete and Ving were laying Leclerc across the rear rack of Ving's unit. Pete was holding a nylon strap to secure Leclerc's body, and Brad couldn't tell if the man was alive or dead.

"Strap him later, Pete! Just hold him!" Pete nodded and climbed aboard the rack, straddling Leclerc's body as Vicky and Chu Hua manhandled Meng into the back seat of Brad's Mrazor. Brad stumbled toward the driver's side, but Vicky gently shouldered him to the passenger side. Bullets were beginning to strike the trees around them as the truck grew nearer, and they could hear the shouts of the men in the truck bed. Jared sprinted forward and leaped onto the rear rack.

"Go!" Brad yelled. Dirt spun from all four wheels as Vicky floored the accelerator and tore off up the goat trail they had so recently come down, Ving right behind her.

* * *

"Somebody tell me what the *hell* is going on!" Fly was hot. She'd been listening to an awful lot of gunfire, explosions and yelling, but no one had bothered to tell her a damned thing and her gut was twisted into knots.

"Is the Big Bird in the air, Fly?" Brad asked tiredly.

"Of course it is. Now you want to tell me what's going on?" she retorted.

"Tell them to bring it in, we're coming home, plus two."

"The girls... You got the girls, both of them?"

"Yes, we have the girls."

"Tell the medic on board to prepare for three casualties needing immediate care, Fly," Vicky snapped, "one life threatening, one pretty badly beaten, and one stubborn fool too hardheaded to do what his doctors tell him to!"

"Who—"

"Just tell the Big Bird we'll be there within thirty mikes, Fly, and I'll give you chapter and verse." Brad gave Vicky a sour look. "It's not that bad."

"Tell it to the docs," Vicky snorted, hot tears flowing down her cheeks. "You're lucky you're still alive."

The Mrazors sped down the now familiar trail until they reached the 'improved' road. When they hit the road, Vicky took the Mrazor all the way up to its top speed. There was no more pursuit.

They reached the unimproved strip just as the C-130's wheels touched down, and Vicky drove onto the loading ramp as soon as the big aircraft turned around to take off. Ving pulled in right behind her, and this time the air crewmen didn't say a word as Charlie and Jared strapped down the rear vehicle. Pete carried Leclerc's inert body to a stretcher at the front of the cargo compartment and the medic went right to work, attaching electrodes and sensors. A second medic approached Meng, but Vicky stubbornly insisted that he attend to Brad first. Brad would have argued, but he had passed out the minute he sat back in the canvass webbing seat.

"For the love of God, will somebody please tell me what the hell is going on?"

EPILOGUE

Day 3, Dyess AFB and Dallas, Texas 1217 hours

The C-130 landed at Dyess AFB and taxied to the end of the runway where it stopped, away from prying eyes. There it was met by an ambulance and a shiny new black Dodge. ICE Special Agent Randolph Curtly, dressed in a dark blue suit and wearing aviator sunglasses, stood in front of the Dodge, hands clasped in front of him. Two attendants and a gurney stood beside the open rear doors of the ambulance.

The tailgate lowered with its characteristic whine, and the two attendants wheeled the gurney up the ramp and onto the cargo deck. One of the air crewmen waved them forward to where a medic stood beside a stretcher. The telemetry equipment was still attached to Leclerc and the man was still unconscious. The medic handed the telemetry case to one of the attendants and then hung an IV bag from the pole on the gurney.

"Got room for one more in the meatwagon?" he asked.

"Forget it, bud, I'm not riding home in an ambulance," Brad retorted.

"We've already been over this. You're not going home, sir," the medic said sternly. "You need a hospital and a doctor."

"I—"

"Shut up Brad," Vicky said angrily. "The only reason we didn't land in San Antonio is because you pitched a royal fit. You're going to a doctor and you're going now!"

"I'll go to the hospital in Dallas," Brad growled.

"Better listen to her, buddy." Ving laughed. "Otherwise you might be bunking at my house for the next couple of weeks." He had been worried about his friend all the way from El Salvador. From the look on the young medic's face, it had been touch-and-go with Brad for about half the flight. It had taken two bags of plasma before Brad's vital signs had showed anything remotely resembling normal vital signs. Only then had the medic turned to Meng to dress her wounds and bruises.

"You understand I cannot report this to the media, sir?" Special Agent Randolph Curtly had the good grace to look embarrassed. Fly had contacted him and explained the unusual nature of this 'capture'. He had owed her a debt of gratitude that he'd believed he would never be able to repay, and he'd jumped at the chance to do so. This was not the first time he had 'captured' a wanted international criminal on American soil that, incidentally, was unaware of exactly how he got on American soil.

"Yeah, we get it. That suits us just fine."

Curtly looked at the band of tough looking men and women and wondered how they had managed to capture Leclerc. He had heard Fly rail about this bastard for a couple of years, and his own research had proven to him how truly evil the bastard was. The last he'd heard, Leclerc had some fancy moniker hung on him and had set himself up as a warlord in El Salvador with his own army and a regular fortress. He sighed and followed the ambulance attendants off of the aircraft. Just before they reached the ambulance, he stopped and cuffed the sonofabitch to the gurney, even though Leclerc had not yet regained consciousness.

"No sense taking any chances," he said agreeably to the attendants. "With a little luck this puke won't wake up till we have him in ADMAX!"

* * *

"Is this the guy that jumped you in the hardroom?" Fly asked, handing Brad an eight-by-ten glossy photograph of Lucien Piccard.

"That's the guy," Jessica said. "I cracked his skull with a bottle of Courvoisier."

"Lucien Piccard, Leclerc's number two," Fly said. "He's a psychopath who was with Leclerc in Northern Mali and other equally rotten places. He was imprisoned with Leclerc in Paris and he helped the bastard escape. Been with him ever since and he's every bit as rotten as Leclerc. A natural born follower, but he's shown indications of ambition in the past. I'd bet money he takes over Leclerc's operations in El Salvador since y'all removed the kingpin."

Jessica looked at Fly first in horror then in disgust. "I should have killed him when I had the chance."

Fly gave the pretty blonde an appraising look.

"I wish I could disagree with you, but I can't. Hell, it's my fault. I should have included Piccard's dossier in the files I gave you." She turned back to Brad.

"So, how did you like my little toys? Did they help you?"

"They were amazing, Fly, and, yes, we would have been screwed without them. I just hate that we didn't recover that damned drone."

"The drone can be replaced, Brad. It's only money."

"It wasn't just the drone, Fly. The knowledge you brought to the table was detailed and accurate, and when the chips were down, you knew what would be important to us without us having to tell you." He glanced over at Vicky, who nodded slightly and smiled.

"I'd like to offer you a job, Fly. How would you like to equip and set up a comm center like yours here at the ranch? I can offer a virtually unlimited budget."

"Sounds good, Brad, but who you gonna get to run it for you?"

"I ... we ... were hoping you would consider coming to work for us full time..."

Fly grinned. "I thought you'd never ask!"

***** THE END *****

Thank you for taking the time to read TRACK DOWN EL SALVADOR. If you enjoyed it, please consider telling your friends or posting a short review. Word of mouth is an author's best friend and much appreciated. Thank you, Scott Conrad.

EXCLUSIVE SNEAK PEEK: TRACK DOWN WYOMING – BOOK 7

The old C-130 was on a milk run from San Diego to Sherman Army Airfield at Fort Leavenworth, transporting prisoners for long-term confinement at the U.S. Disciplinary Barracks. The aircraft had made several stops to pick up prisoners from the Corps as well as the other services; the cheap-ass U.S. Government was 'saving money' by using collection points to pick up prisoners rather than flying them commercial (even though the prisoners were being charged for the flight). Harlan Taggart was sick and disgusted, as well as humiliated, by the whole process. Fourteen years in the Corps and this is what he got for fighting for his country, doing what he had been trained to do.

The officers and NCOs that had railroaded him out of the Corps were men he had fought beside, men whose asses he had saved on more than one occasion and in turn had saved his bacon as well. Men he'd thought were his brothers. One little ruckus over some raghead that would probably have gleefully cut their throats and the men he thought of as brothers had turned on him. Bastards! He'd show them! He'd show them all! It was survival of the fittest now, law of the jungle, and Harlan Taggart was a master of that jungle...

A Brad Jacobs Thriller Series by Scott Conrad:

TRACK DOWN AFRICA – BOOK 1

TRACK DOWN ALASKA – BOOK 2

TRACK DOWN AMAZON – BOOK 3

TRACK DOWN IRAQ – BOOK 4

TRACK DOWN BORNEO – BOOK 5

TRACK DOWN EL SALVADOR – BOOK 6

TRACK DOWN WYOMING – BOOK 7

Visit the author at: ScottConradBooks.com

Printed in Great Britain
by Amazon